torch red

color me torn

melody carlson

TH1NK Books
an imprint of NavPress®

www.navpress.com

TH1NK is an imprint of NavPress.

TH1NK and the TH1NK logo are registered trademarks of NavPress. Absence of ® in connection with marks of NavPress or other parties does not indicate an absence of registration of those marks.

ISBN 1-57683-531-6

Cover design by David Carlson Design
Cover image: Banana Stock
Creative Team: Gabe Filkey, Arvid Wallen, Erin Healy, Darla Hightower, Pat Miller

This is a work of fiction. The characters, incidents, and dialogues are products of the author's imagination and are not to be construed as real. Any resemblance to actual events or persons, living or dead, is entirely coincidental.

Published in association with the literary agency of Sara A. Fortenberry.

Carlson, Melody.
  Torch red : color me torn / a novel by Melody Carlson.
    p. cm. -- (True colors ; bk. 3)
  Summary: Feeling like she is the only virgin on the planet, a high school junior wrestles with questions about love and sex before ultimately choosing to give herself to God instead of her boyfriend.
  ISBN 1-57683-531-6
  [1. Dating (Social customs)--Fiction. 2. High schools--Fiction. 3. Schools--Fiction. 4. Christian life--Fiction.] I. Title.
  PZ7.C216637To 2004
  [Fic]--dc22

                              2004008125

4 5 6 7 8 9 10 11 / 09 08 07 06 05

Other Books by Melody Carlson

Dark Blue and *Deep Green,* Books 1 and 2 of
TRUECOLORS series (NavPress)

DIARY OF A TEENAGE GIRL series (Multnomah)

DEGREES OF GUILT series (Tyndale)

Finding Alice (WaterBrook)

Looking for Cassandra Jane (Tyndale)

one

MY LIFE IS PATHETIC. *REALLY*. IT'S EMBARRASSING, HUMILIATING, TOTALLY Loserville. I mean I can't even admit this to anyone — outside of my family, that is — but I actually spent this New Year's Eve babysitting. *Babysitting!* Now how lame is that? I mean it was okay when I was thirteen or fourteen and needed to make a few extra bucks. But I am *sixteen*, for Pete's sake. Sixteen and three-quarters to be precise, and I didn't even have a date for New Year's Eve.

And as long as it's time for true confessions, the sorry truth is that I've never even had a *real* honest-to-goodness boyfriend. Oh, a couple of guys have asked me out in the past year, and I actually went out with Clark Harris for a while back in middle school, but then we never even kissed. Now here I am, a junior in high school, soon to be seventeen, and I don't even have a boyfriend. So I ask you, what is wrong with me?

Oh, yeah, I *know* I'm not drop-dead gorgeous like Andrea Boswell (she could be a professional model) or that airhead cheerleader Kirsti Quackenbush, but I'm not exactly chopped liver either. And compared to some girls who date regularly, I'm really not *that* bad-looking. Getting my braces off last fall helped, and I haven't even had that many zits this year. My friend Emily Schuler says I look like Winona Ryder, and I'm thinking she may be on to something since I've got those same kind of dark brown eyes and straight brunette hair—although I'm not into shoplifting.

And I have to admit, there are boys who do give me a second look and have even come on to me at times. But unfortunately they're usually the kinds of boys I wouldn't give a second glance anyway, guys like Spence Harding and Aaron Place. It's not that they're losers, exactly, but they don't really strike me as "boyfriend material." Not that I have a right to be too picky. But I really don't want to go out with a guy who is, shall we say, "second rate." I know that's totally shallow, considering I just spent New Year's Eve babysitting, but I suppose I have higher hopes.

What gives me the right to keep these hopes so high? Well, I suppose that's the problem with being "marginally popular." You see, I kind of hang with a pretty cool bunch of kids. This is mostly due to my best friend, Emily (who is a cheerleader, although I am not). And so I suppose I get this idea that *if* (and that's turning into a pretty big *if* these days) I ever date anyone, it should be someone from within that same circle of friends.

Now, I know this is pretty stupid (did I mention shallow?), but it's like I'm in this trap and I don't really see any way out of it. And you know what really makes it seem totally absurd and crazy, or like I'm on some sort of beat-myself-up trip? Well, there's this one particular guy that I've had this sort of secret crush on for years. His name is Nate Stein, but he's really an outsider. The problem has nothing to do with his looks. In fact, he could possibly pass for Orlando Bloom—not with the blond braids as Legolas in *The Lord of the Rings*, but the way he normally looks with his brown hair and sultry eyes. The problem is that he's really into religion, or so I hear. And for whatever reason, that's just not cool with my crowd.

As a result, girls like Kirsti, or even Andrea and Emily, who actually are pretty nice, would never in a million years give a guy like Nate the time of day. But ever since he and I were in band together back in middle school, I've always thought he was kind of cool (and that was before Orlando became hot). But would I go out with Nate now that I'm in high school? Probably not. Now really, how pathetic is that? I suppose I really am a shallow person. And I probably deserve exactly the kind of life I'm living.

It's just that I've had this brief reprieve during winter break. My dad decided to take our family on a ski trip to Colorado during Christmas, and it was so amazing to be away from all the crud and pressure at school. But now it's time to go back, and the prospect seriously has me down. I get so bummed when I think about the disgusting things that are said in the girls' locker room every single day of the school year. And, as if that's not bad enough, I feel ashamed about how I've turned into such a big fat liar this year.

Now, you must understand that my lies were simply a means of survival, and they were of the variety that should just blow over in time. Instead, they've turned into this thing I just can't seem to shake. I mean it all started out innocently enough. It was early September. We were in the locker room getting dressed after fourth-period PE, and it seemed like every girl had to show off her new Victoria's Secret underwear, or Gap or whatever (although some girls actually clip off the labels, like if their moms bought their "unmentionables" at JCPenney or Wal-Mart). And, as usual, this underwear talk quickly led to other kinds of talk. Okay, sex talk, to be precise.

Now when it comes to sex talk, some girls are subtle and rely more on innuendo (meaning they act like they're saying something big, but you could never really prosecute them based on their actual words). Andrea is an expert at this, as is Emily. But that is only since

7

late last summer, when she actually lost her virginity to her current boyfriend, Todd Barker. Before that, she didn't get involved in this kind of talk at all.

But then there are girls like Kirsti and her best friend, Thea Weller, who don't mind telling all (and I mean *every* skanky detail) to anyone who will listen. And let me tell you, it can get pretty disgusting.

"I just don't see what the big deal is," said Kirsti, who in my opinion has been a tramp since middle school. "It's just like kissing," then she giggled, "only using different body parts."

"Eww!" said Emily as she threw her wet towel at Kirsti. "Too much information!" I tossed Emily an appreciative glance meant to convey, "Thanks for voicing my opinion exactly," as I shimmied into my jeans and quickly buttoned them before anyone noticed that I wasn't wearing a thong. (I happen to think they're uncomfortable.)

"Don't be such a prude," said Kirsti as she threw the towel back at Emily. "*Everyone* does it."

"Everyone does *not*," said Andrea as she adjusted what had to be the coolest bra in the locker room that day. Obviously Victoria's Secret and, I suspect, slightly padded, maybe with gel or water or whatever it is they put in those things. I'm glad to say I don't need *that* kind of help.

Thea rolled her eyes at Andrea. "Well, everyone knows you're too much of a goody-goody to have any real fun when it comes to guys. Lucky for you that Jamie doesn't seem to mind."

"Yeah," said Kirsti, "but you'd better watch out, Andrea, or some other babe might come along and give your boy toy a run for his money." Then she made a loud slurping noise and laughed.

"You're disgusting," said Emily as she pulled on her T-shirt.

Kirsti laughed. "Poor Emily," she said with mocking sarcasm. "We shouldn't be so shocking when there are *virgins* around."

Well, all eyes were on Emily just then. Okay, maybe some were on me too. But then I realized that *Emily was no longer a virgin*—which meant I would be the only virgin left in this big-mouthed circle of so-called friends. And I think I actually began to sweat. Fortunately, my deodorant was nearby and I pretended to be completely absorbed in applying layer upon layer to my damp armpits. I did this with such focused perfection that I might've won an audition for a Secret antiper-spirant ad.

"You don't know *everything* about me, Kirsti," said Emily. "Unlike some people, I don't go around blabbering about the private details of my sex life to the entire student body."

"*Yeah*. And we all know *why* you don't."

I glanced over my shoulder at Emily, hoping and maybe even praying that she wouldn't spill the beans. But it was too late.

"Fine," said Emily. "If you *must* know, I'm *not* a virgin anymore. There." She glanced around. "Are you happy now?"

Thea put her arm around Emily's shoulders and smiled, and I could tell by her expression that she already knew about Emily's little secret. Still, it was weird the way Thea looked sort of like this proud mother, like Emily had just learned to ride a bike. Or maybe it was like they were in some special club together, with a secret handshake and everything. And then there was Emily, just smiling like she'd received a national honor or college scholarship or maybe even the Nobel Peace Prize. I just stared at them in amazement.

"Emily has officially joined the ranks of womanhood," Thea announced to everyone within earshot in the locker room. Several girls clapped and cheered.

"No way," said Kirsti.

"Way." Emily firmly nodded.

Kirsti frowned at Thea now. "How come you never told me?"

Thea put a finger to her lips then winked at Emily. "Sworn to silence."

"I still don't believe it." Kirsti's eyes narrowed as she turned back to Emily.

"Whatever." Emily just shrugged.

"You and Todd really did it?" asked Andrea.

"Well, it wasn't me and Zoë!" Emily laughed and nodded in my direction. *Thanks a lot,* I was thinking. I mean not only did that stupid comment make me look totally lame, it was a reminder to the other girls that I was still there and, worse than that, *still* a virgin. Worst of all, I was now the *only* virgin in our group—perhaps the *only* virgin in our entire school, maybe even the planet. As I tugged on my sock, I vaguely wondered if there might be some tribe out on a deserted island somewhere that might pay good money for a real honest-to-goodness virgin. Perhaps I could be used as a sacrifice somewhere to appease a volcano god or something.

"So it's just Zoë now," said Thea in what actually sounded like a sympathetic voice. "The only one left." She patted me on my head as I tied my shoe. "Our little girl."

Well, *that* just got me. So right then and there I decided that the only way out of this thing was to lie—simply and believably. And so I did.

I looked right up at Thea and, using my best poker face, told a whopper. "What makes you think *that*?"

"Huh?" Now Andrea turned around and looked at me with wide eyes. "Really? You too?"

Our area of the locker room got a lot quieter and I felt my friends all staring at me now. Without even blinking, I returned their looks, avoiding Emily's eyes completely. I mean if anyone could blow my cover, it would be my best friend. Just the same, I decided to risk it.

I nodded at Andrea and then shrugged as if it were nothing. "Yeah, it's no big deal."

"No way," said Kirsti as she sat down on the bench beside me. "You're making this up, Zoë."

I rolled my eyes at her. "Yeah, like I would make this up."

"When?" demanded Thea. "With who?"

"Last summer," I lied like an expert. "Remember when I went to California to visit my grandma?"

"No way," said Kirsti again. "You met a guy in California?"

I smiled and nodded. "Yeah. A surfer."

"No way!" shrieked Kirsti. "You did it with a surfer dude?"

"I don't believe you," said Thea. "What's his name?"

"Daniel Englewood," I said without even blinking an eyelash. It was actually the name of a little neighbor boy that I'd babysat a couple of times while staying at my grandma's house, which, by the way, wasn't even close to a beach. "He was tan and blond and really buff." Then I actually sighed as if the memory was making me light-headed. "Daniel was so incredibly cool. I really miss him."

"Way to go," said Kirsti, patting me on the back.

"Yeah," agreed Thea, apparently convinced. "Was he good? Did you do it on the beach?"

"Oh, yeah." I stood and looked at Thea. Emily would see right through me. "But it was more than just the sex, you know. He was really nice too. We were together the whole time I was in California. We promised to write."

"Do you love him?" asked Andrea.

I pretended to consider this. "I'm not sure. But he was a cool guy—a great first, you know."

It wasn't until Emily gave me a ride home later that she questioned my little story. "You never told me about this Daniel guy, Zoë," she said as she drove away from school.

I just shrugged and looked out the window. "Everyone has some secrets."

"But I'm your best friend. I told you all about Todd, practically the next day."

"Well, that was different. You and Todd had been going together a long time. I guess I was a little embarrassed about my fling with Daniel, since I'd just met him, you know, and he lives so far away."

Emily didn't say much after that, but I sensed that I'd hurt her feelings. I even considered telling her the truth, but somehow I couldn't make myself do it. And so for the next few months, I engaged in the locker-room talk a bit more, just so I could be believable. Oh, I never actually said anything too specific when it came to sex. I followed Andrea and Emily's leads by remaining slightly elusive and aloof. But I'd sometimes laugh at Kirsti's off-color jokes and then I'd just roll my eyes at Thea's sleazy descriptions of her latest sexual exploits. But all the time I just kept thinking that I didn't fit in, that I would never fit in.

So now that it's time to go back to school again, it seems more painfully obvious than ever that (1) I don't even have a boyfriend, (2) I am living a complete lie, and (3) I am the last remaining virgin on the planet.

two

DESPITE MY NEW YEAR'S RESOLUTION TO BE MORE HONEST, I HAVE ALREADY
contrived a story about what I was doing on New Year's Eve.
Pathetic, I know. But what's a girl supposed to do? I was just thinking through the details when I was summoned from my first-period
class to go to the office.

Now, as I walk down the mostly deserted hallway toward the
office, I'm not feeling too concerned. I suspect that I've simply been
called down to help with a new student. That's because I'm on H.S.
(Hospitality Squad). It was really Emily's idea to sign up for this
back when we were sophomores, and she talked me into signing up
with her. Then she got too busy with her other activities, but I realized that I actually enjoy it, and so I'm still doing it. Besides, it's a
way to get out of class now and then. I guess I'm a fairly outgoing
person, and I've discovered that I like making new kids feel comfortable. At least for a while. It's not like I take responsibility for
what happens with them later. I mean I don't have to sign on to be
their best friend or anything. But it's kind of fun to show them
around and help them find their classes on their first day.

It turns out that I am exactly right. "Her name is Shawna Frye,"
Mrs. DeWalt informs me, "and she just transferred here from Jackson
High."

"Okay." I nod and look around for this girl. Usually Mrs. DeWalt just introduces me and that's that.

"She's in the waiting area," explains Mrs. DeWalt. "I just wanted to tell you that she seems a little down, Zoë, and I thought maybe you could go the extra mile to make her feel more at home here. Maybe introduce her to some of your friends?"

I kind of frown, thinking this is a little out of the norm, but then I just shrug. "Yeah, sure, I guess I could do that."

Mrs. DeWalt smiles. "Thanks, Zoë. I knew you'd be the right girl for the job."

Then we go out to the office foyer and she introduces me to a pretty girl who's wearing a very cool outfit. But I immediately see what Mrs. DeWalt is talking about. This girl definitely looks bummed about something. Maybe having to switch schools. Anyway, I decide that I'll go out of my way to be really nice to Shawna.

"What year are you?" I ask as we begin to walk down the hall.

"Junior."

"Me too," I say in my most cheerful voice. "It must be hard to move in your junior year."

"Yeah," she answers in a glum voice.

I make my best attempts at small talk as I show her the cafeteria, the classroom wings, the girls' gym, and finally her next class, which happens to be the same as mine, but this girl seems determined not to be cheered up.

"And this is English lit," I finally tell her as we go into our second-period class. I nod to the old guy up front. I've heard they've tried to force him to retire, but he won't give in. "Mr. Franklin comes across as kind of grouchy at first," I whisper to her as we find seats. "But he's really not so bad."

Then Shawna sort of smiles. "I guess you could say the same thing about me."

"Hey, don't worry about it." We sit next to each other. "It must be a drag changing schools."

She nods. "Yeah. It's kind of hard."

Then Emily and Andrea come into the classroom and I quickly introduce them to Shawna. To my relief they both smile and even welcome her to our school.

I pretty much hang with Shawna all morning and even invite her to join me and my friends for lunch. I'm thinking that she's really a lot like the rest of my friends and actually seems to fit in pretty well. But I'm a little worried about girls like Thea and Kirsti. I mean Shawna is cool and everything, but she seems a little quiet and I'm not sure how she'll react to their big mouths.

"Where are you from?" asks Kirsti.

"Jackson," Shawna answers as she sticks a straw into her diet soda.

"My cousin goes to Jackson," Andrea says. "Maybe you know him."

Shawna kind of frowns now, like maybe she doesn't want to talk about this, or maybe it's depressing her.

"I think it's been hard on Shawna," I say quickly, "I mean moving in the middle of the year." I hope that Andrea will catch my drift. But unfortunately she doesn't.

"His name is Caleb Andrews," she continues.

To my relief, Shawna smiles. "Oh yeah. I know Caleb," she says. "We even went out a few times last year."

"Really?" Andrea nods with approval. "I think he's pretty popular over there."

"Yeah," says Shawna. "He's a cool guy. And nice too."

Well, that seems to settle it with Andrea. It's like she's completely accepted Shawna now. And if Andrea accepts someone, everyone else usually just follows along. Shawna tends to stick pretty close to me throughout the rest of the day, and I don't really mind. In fact, I think I'm really starting to like this girl. After she lightened up I could see that she's pretty funny. And she wasn't even offended by Thea's and Kirsti's locker-room stupidity. Let me tell you, they were a little out of hand today. Fortunately for me, they were so busy yakking about *their* New Year's Eve that they never even asked about mine.

After school, Shawna offers me a ride home.

"Good idea," says Emily, my "sometimes ride." "I mean since I've got cheerleading practice today."

"I used to be a cheerleader," says Shawna in a flat voice.

"Too bad you moved here too late to try out," says Andrea. "Maybe next year."

"Yeah. Maybe."

Then I remember that today is tryouts for the spring play. "Hey, I'd love a ride, Shawna, but I was going to try out for the play this afternoon."

"Yeah," says Emily, "Zoë is our drama queen."

"I am *not*."

"Yes, she is," insists Andrea. "She's really good too. You should've seen her in *A Midsummer Night's Dream* as Puck last fall. She was totally amazing."

Now I'm feeling slightly embarrassed, although I don't particularly mind the praise. Okay, maybe I am a little egotistical when it comes to my acting. "Well," I say with a shrug. "I suppose I was okay."

"I was in a play once," says Shawna.

"Hey, maybe you'd like to audition too," I suggest. "I mean I know you're not in drama class, but maybe you could change your schedule if you're interested."

"I guess I could check it out," she says. "Do you mind if I tag along?"

"Of course not."

As we walk toward the auditorium, I tell Shawna about Mr. Roberts. "He's really cool," I explain. "One of my favorite teachers."

"But he had you guys do *A Midsummer Night's Dream*? Shakespeare sounds kind of boring to me."

"It wasn't at all like you'd think. Mr. Roberts found this contemporary version of the play. It started out with us at a slumber party. Really, it was pretty cool."

"Oh."

"And Mr. Roberts wouldn't tell us what the spring play is going to be. He said it was going to be a big surprise."

I am surprised to see how many kids are sitting in the auditorium. Usually drama tryouts aren't this well attended. But today there are tons of kids and suddenly I feel a little worried, like maybe I won't get such a good part.

"We have something different in mind for the spring play," begins Mr. Roberts from the stage. "Miss Lynnwood wants to partner with me to put on a musical."

A simultaneous groan comes from the section where we drama kids are sitting, and even Shawna looks disappointed.

"A musical?" says Casey Renwick.

"Now don't start wigging out," says Mr. Roberts. "I think we can make it a lot of fun."

I'm not entirely convinced. He hands the microphone to Miss Lynnwood, and I notice that he seems to look at her a bit longer than necessary. "I think he has a crush on Miss Lynnwood," I whisper to

17

Shawna, and she nods. I must admit that Miss Lynnwood is really pretty, but I just don't see how that translates into this sudden need to do a musical.

Somehow Miss Lynnwood manages to convince us that a musical isn't a totally lame idea. She tells us how it will probably raise a lot of money for the drama department and how it'll be great to have more kids involved, since even the school orchestra and dance team plan to participate.

"It's a big production, and we need dancers, actors, singers, musicians, set makers, wardrobe, and makeup," she pauses, almost breathless. "And my choir kids already know some of the choruses."

That's when I look around the auditorium and notice that Emily's boyfriend, Todd Barker, is sitting in the front row, right next to Justin Clark, who is like the best-looking guy in Hamilton High, not to mention the star of last season's football team. We're talking a guy who's really tight as well as totally cool. I can't even believe these guys are actually here, although I do know that they're both in choir.

Well, suddenly I'm thinking that maybe this musical business won't be so bad. Especially since I just heard that Justin broke up with Katy Abernathy during Christmas break.

"Not bad," whispers Shawna, and I realize that she's caught me gaping at Justin Clark like a love-struck moron. Man, I just hope I'm not drooling!

I give her a little smile and nod.

"What's his name?"

I tell her, then stupidly mention that he's available, but she assures me that she won't interfere. "He's not really my type," she whispers. "But that guy sitting next to him sure is."

"Yeah, Todd's pretty cute," I tell her. "But he's going out with

Emily." I don't mention that Emily is my best friend and I'm pretty protective of her.

"Oh." Shawna looks disappointed.

Then suddenly Mr. Roberts is announcing the title of the musical that he and Miss Lynnwood have chosen, and it's *Oklahoma!*

"Isn't that some corny old movie they made about a hundred years ago?" someone asks.

"Don't be too quick to judge," says Miss Lynnwood. "It's actually got a lot about relationships and sexual tension."

This makes us laugh, and Miss Lynnwood looks slightly embarrassed.

"We've got some videos of the Hollywood version that can be checked out," says Mr. Roberts as the audition scripts are passed around.

And suddenly we're breaking up into groups (dancers, singers, actors, and whatnot), and Mr. Roberts announces that those trying out for speaking parts have about forty minutes to rehearse some lines before tryouts officially begin.

He explains who the main characters are, and I decide to try for the part of Laurey Williams (the girl's romantic lead). To my dismay, Shawna decides to try out for the same role. But I don't let her know as we practice our lines together—we're supposed to do a romantic scene with the lead guy, whose name is Curly. And suddenly it's time to try out.

I feel about as nervous as usual until I realize that we're not only doing lines, but that we're also expected to sing! And while I'm not the worst singer in the world, I'm not exactly good. I mean I can carry a tune, and I like to sing in the shower or along with a good CD when no one's around, but to stand there on the stage and actually sing in front of all these kids! That's a little over the top. And to make matters worse, Miss Lynnwood expects us to sing "The Star-Spangled Banner"!

I cringe as I hear Casey miss a note, and I figure that she's not going to be too much competition now. But suddenly it's my turn and I feel like I'm going to pass out.

"Break a leg," says Shawna with a wink.

So, suddenly I find myself on the stage, and playing opposite me (as Curly) is Todd Barker. Well, at least that makes me feel more comfortable, since Todd's a good friend, and I must admit that I do my lines pretty well, and I even manage to pull off a pretty good Oklahoma accent (or so I hope). And then it's time to sing. *Well,* I tell myself, *you can do this, Zoë. Just give it your best shot.* So I step up to the piano, where Miss Lynnwood is accompanying, and do my best. And it's really not so totally horrible and a couple of kids even clap.

"My voice could probably use some work," I say apologetically to Miss Lynnwood.

"That was pretty good," she assures me with a smile, and I feel a little bit hopeful.

Then Todd sings and I can't believe how good his voice is, not to mention he exudes confidence. I can't wait to tell Emily what a great job he did today. I feel certain he'll get the guy's lead.

Several other girls audition for Laurey's role, and Becca Carter from choir does a great job singing, but she doesn't really seem to have much spark when it comes to the lines. And then it's Shawna's turn and I feel nervous for her. I mean what must it feel like to not only be the new girl, but to also try out for a play—one where singing is involved? I hope she doesn't embarrass herself.

Then to my total amazement, she not only does the lines perfectly *and* believably, but she has a fantastic singing voice. The whole auditorium gets really quiet while she's onstage, and then everyone claps when she's finished.

"Well, well," says Mr. Roberts as he walks up to her with a big smile. "That was a pretty good performance, especially considering this is your first day at Hamilton High."

Everyone is congratulating her as if she already has the part, and I am feeling a mixture of things. Like kind of jealous, since I know she just aced me out of the part of Laurey, but I'm also glad for her because she looks truly happy for the first time today.

The tryouts seem to go on and on, and I sit in the back of the auditorium and probably look like I'm sulking. I guess I just feel confused, like where do I fit in now that Shawna has stolen the show? Then Mr. Roberts announces that auditions will have to continue tomorrow. I slip out a side door, trying to avoid Shawna and dialing my mom on my cell phone as I go. Mostly I just want to get out of here. Maybe I won't come back to auditions tomorrow. And if Shawna asks why I blew off her offer for a ride, I'll just act like I forgot. I mean I *used* to know how to act.

three

IF THERE'S ONE THING I AM, I GUESS IT'S RESILIENT. I'M KIND OF LIKE
Teflon, the way things can just slide off me sometimes. And I suppose
that's how I feel the next day. Like, hey, I'm not going down this easily. And so, at the end of the day, I go to the play auditions again. But
after a while I start feeling discouraged again and suddenly I wonder
why I even bothered to come. I mean I'm watching Shawna up there
reading lines with guys like Justin and Todd, and I start coming a
little unglued. It's like she totally owns the show. Finally I take a seat
toward the back and just sit there and wonder what hit me.

"How's it going, Zoë?"

I turn to see my old band buddy Nate Stein slipping into the
seat next to me.

"Hey, Nate." I try to smile. "What are you doing here?"

"I thought I'd try for one of the singing roles," he says. "Just for
fun."

"Well, you've always been musical. Do you still have your band?"

"Sort of. Our best drummer graduated and went off to college
last year. But we've got a new guy who's been jamming with us. He
seems to have some potential."

I nod and try to look interested. And I am. Well, sort of. I suppose I'm somewhat amused that Nate actually took the time to come

23

talk to me. But mostly I'm just feeling sorry for myself right now. And I'm just about ready to slip out the back door and pretend like I have absolutely no interest in being in this totally lame musical.

"Your new friend is really something," he continues. "That really took a lot of nerve for her to get up there on her first day. And she looks even more comfortable with it today."

I nod.

"Zoë," he begins, sounding a little hesitant. "It's probably none of my business, but I think you should try out for another part."

I turn and study him, wondering what he could possibly know about something like this. I mean what is he? Some kind of *Oklahoma!* expert?

"It's just that I've been watching the auditions and I really think you'd be a good Ado Annie."

"Ado Annie?" I frown at him. Like what is that?

"I heard Mr. Roberts saying it's the second-best role for girls. I nabbed an audition script, and it sounds like she's slightly comedic, and I heard Miss Lynnwood saying that whoever plays that part doesn't even have to sing that well."

"Thanks a lot."

He grins now. "Hey, you weren't that bad." Then he hands me a new script. "Take a look, Zoë. I bet you'd be perfect."

So I read through it and suddenly I'm thinking this Ado Annie chick sounds like fun.

Once again, the tryouts seem to drag on forever, but I let Mr. Roberts know that I want a chance to try this other role, and finally I am invited onstage to audition for Ado Annie.

To my relief I actually manage to get a couple of good laughs with my lines (I think Nate might be behind this), and then I go back and sit down, feeling certain that I could've done it better. But then I decide that I don't really care how this thing goes. Maybe I can paint scenery or help with costumes. I mean there's more to producing a play than just being onstage.

"We'll post a list tomorrow," Mr. Roberts promises as everyone begins clearing out of the auditorium.

"I'm sure you got the lead," I say to Shawna as we go out the door.

She just shrugs. "Oh, I don't know."

"Don't be ridiculous. You were totally amazing!"

"Really?" She actually seems unconvinced.

I sort of laugh. "Hey, I'm not making this stuff up. And I think everyone else is pretty sure you'll get the part too."

"Are you mad at me?"

I firmly shake my head. "Not at all. I'm happy for you. And now I'm hoping I'll get the part of Ado Annie. She sounds like a real character to me."

"You were totally great as Ado." Shawna takes her keys from her purse. "Do you want a ride home?"

I can tell by the tone of her voice that she's thinking about yesterday. "Sure," I say. Then I smack myself in the forehead like I just remembered something. "That's right, you were going to give me a ride yesterday. Man, I just totally forgot."

She smiles now. "That's okay. I figured that was probably what happened."

So I suppose I'll have to think of a different resolution for this new year. Well.

As Shawna drives me home, she asks about Emily and Todd's relationship. Like, are they really that serious? And how long have they been going out? And didn't I think Todd was really hot? Stuff like that.

"Look," I finally say. "I can't tell you what to do, Shawna, but you need to understand that Emily is my best friend, and out of respect for Emily, I'm strongly suggesting that you keep your distance from Todd."

She nods. "Yeah. You're probably right. I was just curious about how serious they are. And Todd seems cool with being friends with me."

"Well, I'm sure he likes you. And if he gets cast as Curly, which seems pretty likely, you guys will be spending a lot of time together." Hint-hint. Seriously, I want to know how she plans to handle this.

"Don't worry, Zoë. I promise not to seduce him or anything." She grins as she pulls her car into my driveway.

"I'm sure we'd all appreciate that." I smile. "Thanks for the ride."

"Thanks for inviting me to audition!"

* * *

By the end of the week, I decide that Miss Lynnwood actually had the right idea to do a big musical like this. Already it's way more fun having all these other kids around. It's like this nonstop party. Oh, we have to work, of course. And it's a lot harder than usual, since our parts include lots of singing and dancing. But it's turning out to be really fun.

As expected, Shawna was cast as the innocent Laurey Williams, the sweet golden-haired farm girl. Of course, Todd Barker is Curly, the true-blue hero. And I am happy to be playing Ado Annie, a silly sort of girl who chases after anything in pants. But, here's the amazing thing: My main romantic interest is being played by none other than Justin Clark, and we even get to kiss! Oh, life is good.

I also think it's rather ironic that Nate Stein ended up being cast as this Persian peddler, who's also one of my love interests (rather, Ado's). It's ironic, I mean because he's the one who talked me into auditioning for Ado. We have some kissing scenes too. And while I'm sure that Nate has no idea that I've always had a sort-of crush on him, I think it's pretty interesting that I have love scenes with both him and Justin. Of course, my personal interest is leaning toward Justin now. I mean he is so good-looking. Go figure: Only a few days ago I was whining and complaining about the lack of boys in my life.

Miss Lynnwood was right on about the "sexual tension" — there really is a lot of romance and kissing going on in this play. At least in the scenes that we're starting with, which happen to be dance scenes. I guess we'll work on the rest later.

Shawna and I borrowed the *Oklahoma!* movie and watched it a couple times over the weekend. I'll admit it's pretty corny but kind of funny too. But what's even funnier is how many of the kids in the cast seem to be pairing off already. It's like we're really getting swept away by this whole romance thing. And, as it turns out, I think Justin is getting into it too. We've already rehearsed one dance scene where we kiss, and I must say I think I saw stars (or maybe it was the stage lights). Anyway, it was so awesome that I nearly forgot my lines. But I made a good recovery. Anyway, I'm thinking this is turning out to be all right!

Of course, I don't let on to Justin that kissing him is any more than an act for me. I mean how unprofessional would that be? Even so, I suspect that he enjoyed the kissing just as much as I did. Maybe even more.

We're doing that same scene again today. And believe me, I've already brushed my teeth, applied lip gloss with a teeny hint of fruit in it, and am ready for the fun to begin. Of course, Mr. Roberts has instructed us in how to give fake screen kisses, where you don't actually touch lips. He's also made it perfectly clear that there's no need to really kiss at all, especially during rehearsal, but most of the kids are pretty laid back about the whole thing, like we'd all feel silly *refusing* to kiss someone. All of us except for Casey Renwick, that is, who wastes no time making it perfectly clear that she won't be kissing anyone, even though she's playing old Aunt Eller and wouldn't be doing any kissing anyway.

"I'm saving my first kiss until I'm engaged," she announces to everyone within earshot. Casey makes no secret of the fact that she's "a strong Christian" and believes that it's wrong to date. Period. Pretty extreme, if you ask me. I mean people are entitled to believe what they want, and I'm all for freedom of religion, but Casey seems determined to convince the entire planet that her way of thinking is the only way.

"She's *so* weird," Shawna says to me right after a brief sermon on why Shawna shouldn't really be kissing Todd during rehearsal. I kind of have to agree with Casey on this, because it does worry me that Shawna *is* kissing my best friend's boyfriend—even if they are just acting. I suppose I shouldn't be so concerned, since Emily has assured me that she's not the least bit worried. Well, I sure wouldn't be as relaxed as Emily is, but then again, this isn't really my problem.

Right now my biggest concern is Justin! I mean I can tell he's interested in me, but "we" just don't seem to be moving along like I'd hoped. It's like he's holding back, and I wonder if it's because he was hurt by his breakup with Katy. Anyway, I plan to ask him about what happened. Like everyone else, I've heard a variety of stories, but I'm not sure which one is true. And if it turns out that Katy's story is true (meaning she was actually the one who jilted him), well, I may have to rethink my approach. I mean it's not like I want to catch Justin on the broken-hearted rebound or anything. At least I don't think I do. On the other hand, maybe it's better than nothing.

Okay, I'm sounding pretty desperate.

Right now Justin and I are sitting on this big wooden crate, off in the wings, just waiting for our next cue. I swing my legs back and forth, hoping to look less interested than I feel. Then I take in a slow breath. "So, Justin, do you think you and Katy will ever get back together?"

He turns and looks at me, kind of curious, like he's trying to figure out what I'm really getting at here. But he just slowly shakes his head. "I sure hope not."

I nod and attempt to look very empathetic, instead of like yelling, WHOOPEE! I act like I know how it feels to get out of a bad relationship, which is what I'm assuming since he doesn't seem interested in getting back into it. "Still," I continue. "It's kind of rough breaking up with someone, isn't it? I mean especially after you've gone together for a while. Weren't you guys dating for a pretty long time?"

"Not that long. We only started going out last fall."

"Oh." Now I turn my attention back to the stage, where Shawna and Todd are being taught a tricky step by one of the dance-team members. Shawna is way better on her feet than Todd, but she's being nice and patient, even though he keeps stepping on her feet. They're laughing a lot and seem to be having a pretty good time.

"Are you going with anyone, Zoë?"

I turn back to Justin and pretend not to be surprised at his question. "No."

"Why not?"

I smile now. "Just waiting for the right guy, I guess."

Now he smiles. And, let me tell you, he has the best smile. His dark eyes just seem to light up his whole face when he smiles. It's funny, he and I could probably pass for brother and sister with our

29

coloring—both brown-eyed brunettes. But trust me, I don't feel the least bit like his sister.

Suddenly it's time for our scene, and he grabs my hand and we jump off the crate and head for the stage. It's also a dancing scene, or sort of—my character is supposed to be both clumsy and funny—so we both just sort of bumble along. Then finally we get to kiss. And, man, do we kiss! Some of the kids offstage even start to whistle and cheer.

"All right, all right," says Mr. Roberts in a loud voice. "You kids are getting far too carried away with your kissing scenes. I think we'll just nix them altogether from now on. At least during practice."

A few kids make some complaining noises, while others just laugh. And I can feel my cheeks getting red. But Mr. Roberts is already calling up the next scene.

"Come on," says Justin as he pulls me by the hand off the stage. We go back behind some of the old sets and he puts his arm around me and pulls me close to him. "I think Mr. Roberts is all wrong," he tells me in a quiet voice. "I think we need to practice that kissing scene one more time."

I smile and lean into him and am instantly swept away by a long and passionate kiss. Much better than the one on stage. And so we stay back there a while, practicing a bit more. Until I hear someone yelling for us to come out for the group dance scene.

I feel kind of flushed and slightly embarrassed as we emerge. I can tell by the looks and sniggers that some of the kids know exactly what we've been up to. But then I just hold my head high and figure, who cares what they think?

After play practice is over, Justin comes over to where I'm standing with Shawna and calls me aside. "You going to the game tomorrow?"

I kind of shrug, like I'm not really sure, although I do plan on going even if it's by myself.

"Well, you want to go with me?"

I smile. "Sure, Justin. That sounds great."

He looks relieved, and I wonder if he actually thought I might turn him down. Yeah, you bet! Then I give him directions to my house and turn around and give Shawna the biggest grin.

"Cool," she says in a quiet voice, not blowing my attempt to appear nonchalant.

We begin to giggle as soon as we're outside. "I can't believe it!" I tell her. "Justin actually asked me out!"

"He's such a hottie too," she assures me as we get into her car. "I was about ready to go after him myself."

I turn and look at her. "Seriously?"

"No." She laughs as she starts the engine. "Just jerking your chain, Zoë. Don't be so gullible."

Then I laugh too. Suddenly I almost don't care if she decides to go after Todd now. I mean I know that sounds totally disloyal to Emily. But then Emily doesn't seem all that concerned about it anyway. Or else she's just super-confident. Not anything like me. I mean there is *no* way I'd want someone as pretty and talented as Shawna going after *my* guy. Like he's my guy already. Ha! Well, who knows? It could happen!

four

JUSTIN IS SUCH A TOTAL GENTLEMAN. I MEAN HE'S THE KIND OF GUY WHO opens the door for you and treats you like you're something special. Very cool.

By the time we get to the game, I feel like a princess. Okay, that's probably overstating it. But that's just how he makes me feel. Of course, it doesn't hurt that I wore a great new pair of jeans (after exchanging a pretty lame Christmas present that Aunt Linda got for me) that looked totally awesome on me. Believe me, I took my time getting dressed. My mom says she can't figure out how it can take me so long to get dressed when all I'm wearing is jeans and a T-shirt and jacket. But she just doesn't get it.

I mean the T-shirt has to look just right—not too long, not too short—and it needs to fit just so. And then there's picking out the perfect belt and deciding which shoes look best. Tonight it was boots. Really, it's just not as simple as it looks. But, after a couple of hours and a totally ransacked closet, I finally got it together just right. And I could tell that not only Justin but also some of my friends were glancing at me like I was looking good. Huge relief. What if I'd looked like a dog on my very first date with Hamilton High's coolest guy?

Even so, I do feel a bit self-conscious as I walk across the gym floor with him. But that is mostly due to the fact that Justin and I are like *the latest news*. Emily gives me a subtle thumbs-up, since I'd already clued her in to what was going on. But I'd also asked her *not* to tell *anyone*, and being a good trustworthy friend, she didn't. I can tell she didn't by the expressions of shock. Kirsti Quackenbush even drops a pom-pom she's so stunned. But then Kirsti is pretty good friends with Katy, and it's possible that she thinks I shouldn't be going out with Justin now. Or maybe Kirsti is bummed that she missed her own opportunity.

I see Shawna sitting up on the bleachers with some of the drama kids and I'm happy that she's fitting in so well. Todd's with them, but at least he's not sitting right next to Shawna. Then I remind myself, hey, it's not my problem anyway! I've warned Emily several times now. But she just acts like she and Todd are so tight, so committed to each other, that no one could possibly break them up. I cannot imagine having that kind of confidence in a guy. Especially someone as hot as Justin, or even Todd. But then I remember that she and Todd have had sex. And I wonder if *that's* what makes her so sure of herself.

Justin finds us a good seat, and we sit down and start visiting with friends as well as each other, and I'm relieved that he's not one of those guys who brings his girlfriend to a game then just leaves her on her own until it's over. I've seen some guys do that and I think it's totally rude. So I'm sitting here next to Justin, thinking, *all right—now this is the way it's supposed to be!*

"What's up with you and Justin?" asks Kirsti as the dance team does their halftime performance.

"What do you mean?" I act like I'm clueless.

"I mean"—she glances over her shoulder—"are you like going out?"

"We came to the game together." *Like duh, what do you think?*

"So are you like a couple then?"

I just shrug and then wave at Emily and hurry over as if I have something important to tell her.

"Kirsti is totally baffled," says Emily. "It's like she just can't believe it."

I roll my eyes. "Like he's too good for me?"

"Oh, I don't think that's it."

"Or maybe she wishes she'd gotten to him first, since she's temporarily out of a boyfriend."

"Well, knowing Kirsti, that won't last too long. But tell me, how's it going? Do you really like him?"

I nod eagerly. "He is sooo nice, Emily. Right now he's out there getting me a Coke, and you know how long those lines are during halftime."

"Yeah, I've always thought Justin was a good guy." Emily smiles. "I'm so happy for you!"

Then Justin comes back with my drink and we resume our spots on the bleachers and I am feeling like I'm on top of the world. So cool.

But the basketball game seems to literally fly by. And I'm having such a good time that I don't even feel too bad that our team loses, although I do put on the obligatory act. I suppose I am sort of sad, but mostly because the game is over and my date with Justin will soon come to an end.

But then he invites me to go to Chevy's with him and, of course, I agree. I mean why would I want this date to ever end? Chevy's is this new fifties-style restaurant downtown. It's partly owned by Coach Hampton (the football coach) and last fall he talked a lot of his players into hanging out here pretty often. It's kind of funky with all its fifties memorabilia, and sometimes you feel like you should be wearing one of those skirts with a poodle on it, but it's better than nothing. And, believe me, I am totally jazzed to be here tonight.

"What's up with you guys?" asks Andrea when I go to use the bathroom.

"Huh?"

"You and Justin."

"We're together," I say. "Hadn't you noticed?"

She nods. "Of course I noticed. But when did this happen?"

"We started hanging together during play rehearsals." I'm willing to explain, since I really do respect Andrea and actually care what she thinks of me. "We have a lot of scenes together and we just sort of hit it off."

"Cool." Then she pats me on the back.

"Not cool when Katy finds out," says Kirsti. She emerges from one of the stalls.

"But they broke up ages ago," says Andrea.

"But Katy still likes him."

"Like that matters." Andrea puts on some lip gloss.

"Katy told me they were getting back together."

"Doesn't look that way to me," says Andrea.

"I don't really think Justin wants to get back with her," I add. Then Andrea and I leave before Kirsti has a chance to say anything else.

"She's probably just jealous," says Andrea once we're out of the bathroom. "Maybe she thought she'd have a chance."

Suddenly it occurs to me that hanging on to Justin might not be as easy as I'd hoped. But my insecurity melts away when I sit back down at the table across from Justin and see him looking at me. There are lots of kids around and the room is hot and noisy, but for a few seconds it feels like it's just the two of us. And somehow I think this might be the real thing. This might be that big romance I've been hoping and waiting for.

"Want to get out of here?" he asks. I nod.

We go outside and instead of heading for his car, we walk down Main Street, just talking. He is holding my hand and I am so happy that I think I must be dreaming.

"I didn't know what it'd be like, being in the play," he says as we stop to look in the drugstore window. It's set up with a Valentine's Day display of two ice-skating bears surrounded by boxes of candy, stuffed toys, and balloons. Kind of silly, but sort of sweet and romantic too.

"Yeah, I was surprised that so many kids turned out for it," I tell him. "But it makes it more fun."

"I just figured, hey, it's my senior year, why not do something totally different? Mix it up a little."

"I'm glad you did."

"So am I, Zoë." He turns and looks at me now. "Just think what I would've missed." Then he leans down and kisses me. And, naturally, I kiss him back. We stand there in the streetlights kissing like we're starring in some old Hollywood flick. Honestly, I almost expect some old movie star to tap dance down the sidewalk, singing some old funny song. That's how sweet this is.

Then we walk back to his car and climb inside, where we kiss some more and I feel like I'm being swept away. I mean I am feeling things I've never felt before, and Justin is totally in charge of this thing. And it feels like he knows what he's doing.

Then his hand lands in a place that makes me feel uncomfortable and suddenly I am sitting up and sort of pushing him away. He looks startled, then nods as if he understands. "I'm sorry, Zoë." He straightens himself in the driver's seat. "I guess I got carried away."

I start feeling pretty silly. Like maybe I'm totally lame or just immature or maybe I *am* a real prude. Still, it's like whatever was going on—I mean the moment, the magic—well, it's all kind of lost on me now. "I'm sorry," I mutter.

"No, Zoë," he assures me. "It's not your fault. I was just moving too fast." He runs a hand through his dark silky hair. "I mean this is just our first date."

I'm feeling like I can breathe again. "Yeah," I agree. "And it's been really cool. I've had a great time, Justin. My head is spinning."

He laughs as he starts his car. "Yeah, mine too." He turns and smiles at me as he backs out of the parking spot. "But it's not a bad thing."

He puts a good CD in and we both seem to relax as he drives me home. Then he walks me to my door and kisses me one more time, which I find very reassuring, like maybe I haven't scared him off completely.

"Thanks for everything," I tell him as I reach for the doorknob.

"Thank you," he says as he slowly runs his forefinger down my cheek, giving me the good kind of shivers. "Maybe this will become a regular thing with us."

And then we say good-night and I feel like I'm floating on a cloud as I go into my house.

"Out kind of late, aren't you, Zoë?" asks my dad as he emerges from the kitchen wearing his bathrobe and holding a glass of milk.

"Is it that late?" I ask kind of absently.

He looks slightly amused. "Depends on your perspective, I suppose."

Now here's the good thing about being the baby in a family with three daughters: By the time you're old enough to date, Mom and Dad have had plenty of time to loosen up. I mean I can remember this one night, back when I was still in middle school and my oldest sister, Claire, missed her curfew. My parents just totally freaked. I think they actually called the hospital. And when Claire finally came home (only about thirty minutes late as I recall) she was thoroughly lectured then grounded for two weeks.

Next came my sister Amy. Well, she was the wild child and basically drove my parents bonkers by breaking curfews right and left. Amy pretty much did whatever she wanted until I thought both of my parents were going to fall completely apart. My dad's hair actually turned gray during that era. Well, let me tell you, they were so relieved when Amy graduated high school without getting arrested or killed. And they seem to be breathing easier since she went off to college last year. So now I think my parents are pretty much worn out. Or else they figure if Claire and Amy survived, then I probably will too. Whatever it is, I'm finally thankful for being the baby in the family.

"Sorry," I told my dad, "but I had a really great time tonight. And you should be happy to hear that Justin is a total gentleman."

Dad smiles with what appears to be relief. "He seemed like a nice young man."

"Oh, he is, Dad," I assure him. "He really is."

Dad holds up the milk glass. "That's good to hear, honey. Now I better get this up to your mom."

five

BY MONDAY I FEEL LIKE I'VE BEEN ELEVATED A COUPLE OF RUNGS ON THE social ladder. Justin drove me to school and walked me to my locker, and then he even hung with me for a while during lunch.

"So you and Justin are really a thing now?" asks Andrea as we're all getting dressed in the locker room. The area right around us gets quiet and I can tell the other girls are listening in.

"I guess so." I attempt nonchalance and pull on my jeans.

Kirsti leans over and puts her face close to mine. "So, have you done it yet?"

At first I'm confused, then I realize she's talking about sex. Even so, I don't answer.

"Are you kidding?" says Thea. "Zoë's too much like Emily. She'll probably hold out for months too."

Emily just rolls her eyes as she reaches for her sweater. I wish I knew how to be as cool about this as she is.

"She'll lose him then," says Kirsti. "I have inside information that Justin's not one to wait around."

"From Katy?" asks Thea.

Kirsti nods.

"Where is that girl anyway?" asks Emily. "I haven't seen Katy since before Christmas. Is she sick or something?"

Kirsti glances around, I'm sure to see if Mrs. Post, our PE teacher, is nearby. "Haven't you heard?"

Thea smirks as if *she* has.

"Heard what?"

"Katy's been doing a little Hoovering," says Kirsti.

"Huh?" Now this intelligent response comes from me, but I wish I'd kept my mouth shut.

"Katy did some *Hoovering* last week," says Kirsti in this sort of dramatic tone. Feeling like an idiot, I just nod as if I know what she's talking about, which I totally don't.

"You're kidding," says Emily and I can tell she's shocked, but I still don't get what they're talking about.

Kirsti shakes her head. "No one's supposed to know," she says in a quiet voice.

"Then why are you telling *us*?" demands Andrea.

"Emily's the one who asked. Besides, aren't you Katy's friends? I figured you'd want to know. Sheesh, don't get all freaked at me."

"Just because I asked about Katy doesn't mean you have to tell everyone the explicit details of her personal life," says Emily. "I can't believe Katy thinks you're her friend."

"Yeah," agrees Andrea. "You going to practice now, Emily?" And then those two take off and I'm left trying to sort it out.

"Ready to go to play practice?" asks Shawna. I'd forgotten she was here.

I nod as I shove my PE clothes back into my locker. I'm glad to get away from Kirsti and Thea, who are now going on about "how some girls are so sensitive and just need to grow up."

"Do you know what Kirsti was talking about in there?" I ask Shawna once we're out in the breezeway.

She nods. "Of course. Don't you?"

I shrug. "Well, not really."

Shawna turns and looks at me. "You really are pretty naive, aren't you, Zoë?"

Somehow, maybe because she's new here, I don't mind so much that Shawna knows I'm not as "sophisticated" as some of my friends. "I guess so," I admit. "I mean I kind of play along, but half the time I'm not sure what Thea and Kirsti are talking about. Or if I do know, I think it's pretty gross. But I've learned to play along."

Shawna laughs now. "No wonder you're so good in drama."

"Thanks. I guess." Then I turn to her. "But really, I want to know what Hoovering is supposed to mean."

"Probably that Katy got an abortion." Then Shawna shrugs like it's no big deal.

I feel my eyes growing wide. "You mean she was pregnant?"

Now Shawna looks mad. "Look, Zoë, I don't even *know* this girl. I have no idea whether she was pregnant or not. Or whether she got an abortion. All I'm telling you is that's what Hoovering means." She pauses now. "Sorry, I didn't mean to blast you. But sometimes I get so sick of gossipy girls. Like why can't they just mind their own business?"

I nod. "Yeah, I totally get what you're saying." Then we're at the auditorium and I'm feeling lousy. If it's true—if Katy really was pregnant and really got an abortion—then it's likely that Justin could've been the father. And this just totally freaks me.

I feel Shawna's hand on my arm. "Zoë," she says quietly, "it might not even be true, you know? I mean Kirsti might've just made up the whole thing to get to you."

I nod as I consider this. "Yeah, that's possible."

"Some girls are like that. They just want to mess with your mind."

Now I'm wondering if that might not be the reason Shawna left her old high school. I know where she lives now, and it's not even within our district. I wonder if someone over at Jackson had messed with her or gossiped about her or done some permanent damage. But Mr. Roberts is up on the stage yelling for everyone to get into place, and I realize I'll have to ask her about that later. If at all.

Justin comes over to join me now and I suddenly feel uncomfortable around him. It's like there's this wall between us. I try to smile and act normal, but I can tell that I'm not very convincing.

Finally, just before practice ends, he asks me what's up.

I kind of shrug and look down at my shoes. We have to wear these weird little dancing slippers for practice and they take some getting used to. "I don't know," I finally say.

"I think you do." He pulls on my hand. "Come on, tell me. What's up?"

"Well, I heard something today . . . ," I begin, wondering how I can possibly get these words out.

"About what?"

"About Katy Abernathy . . ."

"Uh-huh?"

"Well, Kirsti said that Katy got an abortion." But I study Justin's face as I say this and I can tell by his raised brows and confused-looking eyes that he is totally shocked.

"What?" he asks in a hushed voice, pulling me farther offstage in case anyone else is listening.

"Kirsti and Thea said that Katy got an abortion during Christmas break."

He runs his hand through his hair then shakes his head and finally says, "No way."

I just shrug. "Shawna thought they might've been making it up, for my sake, you know."

"Man, that's cruel."

"I know."

"Do you believe them, Zoë?" He's looking into my eyes now.

"Well, I figured if Katy was pregnant and got an abortion, you would know about it. Right?"

"Yeah. Definitely."

"And since you seem as shocked as I am, I'm guessing it's not true."

He seems relieved now. "Thanks."

"Are you going to ask Katy about it?"

Now he looks perplexed. "You mean like call her up and say, 'Hey, Katy, did you get an abortion?'"

The way my insecurity shows suddenly embarrasses me. "I guess that'd be pretty lame, especially if Kirsti made the whole thing up."

"Yeah. And kind of insulting too, don't you think?"

I nod. "I guess it's best to just forget about it."

And so that's what we do. We both decide to pretend like we've never heard this stupid rumor. And I believe Justin is telling the truth. I mean he's a pretty good actor and all, but I seriously doubt he could've faked looking as shocked as he did. He was totally stunned and even a little hurt, I think. Which shows me that he's a pretty sensitive guy. And it makes me really mad at Kirsti and Thea for coming up with this crud. It's like they want everyone to be miserable. I just don't get it.

Justin gives me a ride home and even walks me to the door. "So you're okay about everything now?" he asks as we stand on my porch.

"Yeah. Sorry if it seemed like I overreacted. I was just so shocked."

"Me too. It's a sleazy thing for Kirsti and Thea to say about Katy. I mean Katy doesn't mean anything to me anymore, but they don't have to go dragging her name through the mud."

Then he leans down and kisses me and says he'll pick me up for school in the morning. And suddenly it seems like we're back to normal. Although I must admit I don't feel like normal. I feel like I'm flying high.

* * *

Later in the evening Shawna calls. "How'd it all go with Justin?" she asks.

"Fine," I assure her. "He thinks that Kirsti and Thea cooked the whole thing up. Just like you said."

"Yeah, it figures."

"I appreciate you telling me that, Shawna. I might've got upset and said something really stupid to Justin. You helped me to keep a level head."

"Glad I'm good for something."

"Something you said made me curious though . . ."

"About what?"

"Well, it sounded like maybe you'd had a bad experience, like with girls gossiping or whatever. I was just wondering if that's why you transferred from Jackson to Hamilton?"

She took awhile to answer. "Yeah. There were some people determined to make my life miserable. It was time for a fresh start."

"Well, I'm glad. It's been great getting to know you."

"Thanks, Zoë."

We chat a little more then hang up. Now I'm feeling a little guilty because it's like Shawna seems more like my best friend than Emily. But that's probably due to our current activities. Emily's all into cheerleading and I'm into the play. Just the same, I decide to email Emily before I go to bed, just to let her know what Justin said about the stupid accusation. I don't want her to feel like I left her out of the loop or anything.

Or maybe it's because I'm still trying to convince myself of the truth.

six

APPARENTLY ANDREA REALLY LAID INTO KIRSTI AND THEA AT CHEERLEAD-ing practice on Monday. Emily told me that they both promised to watch their mouths a little better. I, for one, am grateful.

Katy was back in school by the middle of this week and the story (which I believe is true) is that she had an appendicitis attack during the holidays. And how rotten is that, to go through an appendectomy and then be falsely accused of having an abortion? Apparently no one has mentioned this nasty little rumor to her. For Katy's sake I'm relieved, but I must admit there's probably a bit of selfishness in my relief. It's not that I don't like Katy, but she's never been terribly friendly to me. I guess I don't really get her. And frankly, I don't even know what Justin saw in her. But then I suppose I don't need to worry about that.

No, I have something totally new to worry about today.

It happened at play practice. A strap on one of my dancing slippers broke after a pretty vigorous dance routine with Nate Stein.

So I excuse myself and hurry off to the wardrobe room in search of a safety pin to fix it. The room is dark—not unusual since we're not really doing much with costumes yet—and I hear this kind of rustling sound. Thinking it might be a rat (last winter a few did serious damage to our costumes), I flip on the light switch and get ready to grab a broom or sword or whatever it might take to fend off the nasty little beast. But it is *not* a rat.

Well, actually it is *two* rats. *People* rats. Mainly, Shawna and Todd rats. And these rats are in a corner of the costume room, doing something only rats would do.

At first I'm not even sure exactly *what* they're doing or who it even is, but it doesn't take long to figure it out. Todd is leaning against the King Lear throne (a prop left over from a performance done several years ago) but when I first see him, I actually think maybe he's having a seizure and needs medical help or something. Then I notice someone else is with him and that's when I realize it is Shawna! And then I get it—I understand what she is doing to him and it makes me so sick that I want to puke all over the *Midsummer Night's Dream* costumes that are piled high in a box right next to me. In my whole life, I've never seen anything so skanky! I feel myself gasp, but Shawna doesn't even turn around. Maybe that's a good thing.

To say I am completely stunned or even grossed out is a total understatement. But, here's what gets me: I am thoroughly embarrassed by their moronic stupidity. I mean my cheeks are flaming like torches. But instead of confronting the rats, I play the mouse's role. I quietly turn off the light, close the door, and then walk away. And when I'm just steps away from the wardrobe room, I run smack into Casey Renwick, which causes me to nearly fall flat on my face.

She actually catches and helps to steady me. "It's time for your next scene, Zoë," she informs me. "Did you get your safety pin?"

I stand up straighter then just mutely shake my head as I rush past her.

Then I run back out to the stage with my strap still flapping around on my right shoe.

"Hurry up, Zoë," calls Miss Lynnwood, and I realize it's my singing number. Like I really want to sing right now!

That's when Casey rushes back onto the stage and, with safety pin in hand, tells me to sit down on a wooden crate. She kneels and attaches my flopping strap back onto my shoe.

"Thanks." I feel like I'm about four years old.

She nods and sort of smiles.

Then Miss Lynnwood hands me the music and starts playing the introduction to my little song about how I love to kiss all the guys. After what I just witnessed, the words to this song just make me want to gag. But somehow I manage to choke it out and Miss Lynnwood actually seems pleased when I'm done.

And suddenly Todd and Shawna are back on the stage, acting like nothing unusual has just transpired in the wardrobe room. I mean they don't seem the slightest bit concerned or even guilty as they practice their next number. And they don't even flinch when I give them both my best you-dirty-rats look. Well, I am just totally fried!

I am glad when Justin offers me a ride home and I am able to avoid Shawna. I mean what am I supposed to do about this? Act like nothing happened, like everything is perfectly fine? Peachy keen? I mean I'd just caught her doing something totally disgusting with my best friend's boyfriend. My best friend, who gave up her virginity to Todd Barker (and keep in mind that Emily told me, back in middle school, that she was going to save herself for her wedding night!), because she thought they had the kind of love that would last forever. Yeah, right!

"What's wrong, Zoë? You seem really quiet."

I just shrug and say, "Nothing." Like I really want to tell Justin about what I saw. You bet!

"Come on. I know something is wrong. Just tell me."

49

"You really want to know what's wrong?" I finally ask him in a totally grumped-out voice, which I immediately regret. I mean it's not like he's the one to blame here.

"Yeah." He glances nervously in my direction. "Did I do something to offend you?"

"No," I assure him. "It's not you." Then I launch into my story about finding the two human rats in the wardrobe room and, without giving graphic details, I manage to convey what the rats were up to. And to my surprise, he just throws back his head and laughs. Like it's some big joke!

"What on earth is funny about *that*?" I demand, ready to ask him to drop me out on the next corner. I mean a girl can only take so much!

But he's laughing so hard he can't even answer. So now I'm not only furious at Todd and Shawna, but I'm feeling seriously irked at Justin too.

"It's *not* funny!"

"I know, I know. It's just funny the way you told it." I can tell he's trying to suppress his laughter.

"But Todd is supposed to be going with *Emily,*" I protest. "Can you imagine how devastated she'll be when she hears about this? What am I supposed to do?"

He's getting more sober now. "I don't know, Zoë. But do you think it's really your business?"

"Emily's my best friend!"

"But don't you think it'll just hurt her to find out about this?"

"Are you saying I *shouldn't* tell her?"

"Maybe."

"Do you honestly think it'll be less painful if she doesn't *know* about it?"

He shrugs. "Well, they say what you don't know can't hurt you."

I firmly shake my head. "Like if you didn't know that a two-ton boulder is about to fall on your head, maybe it will just bounce off?"

"I don't know."

"Or maybe you'll just be dead before you know what hit you?"

"Emily isn't going to be hit by a boulder, Zoë."

I huff and cross my arms. "I thought Shawna was my friend. And I warned her not to get involved with Todd."

"It's not like you could've stopped them, Zoë." He turns down my street now.

"But she should've respected that he was going with someone else."

"People go together. People break up." He exhales loudly almost as if he's exasperated at this whole conversation now. "I mean that's just the way it is."

Now I feel totally deflated, like maybe he's talking about us. "So is that what I should expect, Justin? Are you saying that we'll go together and then just break up?"

We're at my house now and he pulls next to the curb then turns to look at me. His expression is a mixture of sadness and confusion, and I suddenly feel guilty for dragging him through all this Todd-and-Shawna crud with me.

"Look," he begins. "I can't predict the future. I mean I think you're totally cool. And I love being with you and everything. But how do we know what's ahead?"

I sigh. I mean it's not like I'm trying to get some big commitment out of this guy. I know we've only been together for a week. Still, I just like him so much. And I feel really confused right now.

"I'm sorry," I finally tell him. "I didn't mean to dump on you, and I shouldn't take it out on you. I guess I'm just really frustrated at Shawna right now. And I feel like I need to be loyal to Emily, you know. It's confusing."

He nods. "Yeah, and just for the record, I think Todd is a stupid jerk for cheating on Emily like that. I mean Emily is a totally cool girl. Todd's just being a real moron."

Well, at least that was reassuring. "But you really don't think I should tell Emily?"

He shrugs now. "I think it's complicated, Zoë. But I'm sure you'll figure it out."

I sigh again and shake my head. "Yeah, sure."

"You free tomorrow night?" he asks hopefully. "Or do you still plan on being totally bummed over your best friend's cheating boyfriend?"

"That sounds like the title of a really bad song." I smile. "But I think I should be over this by then. Why?"

"Because there's a party I thought you might like to go to with me."

"Sure. Where at?"

He tells me a name that I don't recognize and then explains that the guy is older, and for some reason I suspect it's going to be a party where alcohol is flowing freely, but I agree to go anyway. Okay, I admit to feeling a little uncomfortable about this since my parents usually want to know where I'm going, and so far I haven't felt the need to lie to them. But giving them a name that I don't even recognize is going to raise their suspicions.

Justin walks me to the door with his arm securely around me, pausing to kiss me just long enough to get my heart beating faster.

"Pick you up around seven thirty then?"

"Sure," I tell him. "Can't wait."

* * *

Later that night I get a phone call from Casey, of all people. "What's up?" I ask.

"I just thought I should tell you that I saw it too."

"Saw what?" I ask, but I think I know. I can tell by the tone of her voice.

"You know." She continues with hesitation, as if it makes her uncomfortable to even talk about it. "What was going on in the wardrobe room . . . with Shawna and Todd . . . I saw it too, and I could tell that you were pretty upset about the whole thing, and I just thought, well, if you need to talk or anything, I'm willing, you know."

I sigh, relieved that someone (even if it is Casey Renwick) understands how I'm feeling. "Thanks," I tell her. "Yeah, I was pretty weirded out by that. I mean crud, it was totally disgusting!"

"I know," she says. "Despite what everyone thinks about me, I do realize stuff like that happens. But even so, it's pretty shocking to walk in and actually see it with your own eyes."

"Tell me about it. And if it wasn't bad enough in itself, now I have to figure out what I should do about Emily."

"You mean because she and Todd are supposed to be going together?"

"Yeah, and because she is my best friend. Man, I am so furious at Shawna."

Casey clears her throat now. "Well, as I recall there were *two* of them in there, Zoë."

"Maybe so, but even *you* should know how guys can be such jerks about this kind of stuff. I mean if they can get it they will."

"And that makes them innocent?"

"No, not innocent." I'm feeling irritated now. Like what am I doing talking to Casey Renwick about this stuff?

"Maybe you're suggesting there should be a different moral standard for guys?"

"Well, everyone knows that most guys are just users when it comes to sex and stuff. Not all of them, of course." And I'm thinking that *my* guy is different. Otherwise he wouldn't have backed off on our first date. "It's just a fact that most guys are looking for some action."

"And that makes it okay for the guys?"

"I'm not saying that," I tell her. "I just mean that Shawna crossed a line today."

"So what are you going to do about it?" she asks. "I mean about Emily?"

"I don't know. Justin said that I shouldn't tell her, that it would only hurt her."

"And what do you think?"

"I don't know. Maybe he's right. I mean it's not really any of my business. Maybe I should just try to forget the whole skanky thing."

"Maybe . . ."

But the way she says "maybe" makes me wonder if she actually thinks otherwise. "Okay, Casey." I feel myself giving in now. "What would *you* do?"

There's a long pause, and I start to wonder if she's hung up on me (like maybe I've been too rude) but then she speaks. "I guess I'd have to ask myself how I'd want to be treated if it were me."

"Huh?"

"You know," she continues. "Put yourself in Emily's shoes. What would you want your best friend to do?"

I consider this. "I guess I'd rather know. Yeah, if my boyfriend were cheating on me, I feel pretty certain that I'd want to know."

"That's how I'd feel." Then she laughs. "Well, if I had a boyfriend, which thankfully is *not* the case. See, Zoë," she says in a somewhat self-satisfied tone, "this is exactly why I think we're all better off not dating at all."

"Hey, thanks for calling," I quickly tell her, worried that she's going to start preaching at me again. Like it's my personal fault that Shawna and Todd can't control themselves.

"I just felt like maybe I should," she says. "Like maybe we both needed to talk about it, you know, to kind of process it."

"Yeah," I tell her. "It was sweet of you."

"I guess it was just a God thing," she says. "I'm glad I was listening."

"Yeah," I say, hoping that she won't get going on that now. "I appreciate it."

"Well, you seem like a nice girl and I could tell by the look on your face that you weren't used to that kind of thing."

"Yeah, you could say that."

"But you and Justin are dating now."

"Yeah?" Now I wonder where she's going with this.

"Aren't you a little worried about that, Zoë?"

"Huh?"

"I mean he's kind of got a reputation if you know what I mean. Do you really think—"

"Look, Casey, it was nice of you to call and everything. But I don't think it's right for you to suggest that Justin has a reputation. You don't even know him. And I should think that you, being a Christian and all, wouldn't want to be gossiping about something that you couldn't possibly understand."

Now there is a silence and I'm sure I've offended her. But maybe I don't care.

"Sorry," she finally says. "I didn't mean to be gossiping. I guess I just feel concerned about—"

"I'm a big girl, Casey. I can take care of myself."

"All right. No hard feelings then?"

"Of course not."

Then we both hang up. But now I'm feeling seriously aggravated. What right does she have to make accusations against Justin? It's not like she's ever dated him. Or anyone else for that matter. Maybe she's just jealous. Maybe this whole I-don't-believe-in-dating thing is just a big camouflage for the fact that no guy has ever asked her out.

I try to focus my thoughts on poor Emily. I suppose Casey might be right that Emily needs to know about this. I mean that's how I'd feel if I were in her shoes, which thankfully I am not.

I start to call Emily but then remember she's at an away game tonight. I would've gone myself, but play practice ran late and it would've been impossible to get there in time to see much more than the last few minutes. Besides that, I'm totally exhausted. Doing these rehearsals every weeknight can be draining. But I know it'll pay off. So I decide to email Emily, but I don't tell her anything specific, just that we need to talk ASAP. Then I go to bed, hoping that I won't dream about *Oklahoma!* tonight or, worse yet, those two nasty rats in the wardrobe room.

seven

I WAKE UP TO MY MOM'S VOICE. SHE IS REMINDING ME THAT TODAY IS MY day to help out at the soup kitchen.

"Yeah, yeah." I turn back over in my bed.

"Come on." She pulls back my warm comforter. "You made a commitment, and they're expecting you to be there."

I make a face and groan.

"It's already late, Zoë," she says in her I-mean-business voice. "People are counting on you."

Now, I am not what you would call a religious person—not at all. I mean I only go to church when my parents force me, which is usually only on holidays or when they're feeling particularly bossy or religious themselves. But I do think it's right to help out our fellow man, especially those who are struggling just to survive. And my parents' church, which is this old one that's right downtown, has a soup kitchen on Saturday afternoons. It only runs during the winter months, but somehow my parents talked me into volunteering this year. And so, even though I'd much rather sleep in until noon, I force my weary body out of bed, take a quick shower, pull on my clothes, and stumble downstairs.

"You better hurry," says Mom as she hands me a bagel with cream cheese. "It's almost ten, Zoë."

"Yeah, yeah," I mumble as I head for the back door.

"Don't forget the car keys," she reminds me as she drops them in my other hand.

"Thanks a lot," I mutter as I go out to the freezing cold garage.

"Drive carefully, honey," she calls.

"Yeah, yeah . . ."

I get into Mom's car and carefully back out, reminding myself that one of the perks of working at the soup kitchen on Saturdays is that I get to use Mom's car and she doesn't even mind if I stop by the mall on my way home. And that's exactly what I plan to do, since I still have that gift certificate my grandma in Iowa sent me for Christmas. I'm thinking I'll find something new to wear to the party tonight. To be honest, it's about the only thing that gets me going this morning.

"Hey, Zoë," calls out Pastor Leon as he carries a box of food into the church.

"Hey," I answer with a smile.

"Good to see you."

"Yeah," I say as I hold the door for him. "You too." Okay, it's not totally honest, but polite. I hang up my jacket and reach for an apron.

"I'm glad you're here," he says as he puts the box on the counter. "Mavis said we're going to be really busy because we're a little shorthanded."

"Guess I better get to work then."

"Want to help me unload the van for starters?"

"Sure," I tell him, but the truth is, I'm not that excited about working with Pastor Leon today. Not that he isn't nice. He totally is. But I always feel kind of guilty around him since I so seldom go to church. I'm afraid he might think I don't like him or something.

I follow him back to the parking lot and wait as he pulls a box of canned corn from the back of his van and hands it to me. To be polite, I wait for him to get a box for himself then we walk back toward the church.

"Not much of a churchgoer, are you?" he says.

What did I tell you? "Well . . . uh . . ."

He laughs and that's when I notice he has this really cool laugh, kind of deep and hearty and warm. Just like you'd expect from a big African-American guy like him. "Don't worry," he tells me, "I'm not going to lay some big guilt trip on you. I just thought I'd mention it in case you were feeling uncomfortable."

"Actually, I do feel kind of bad about that."

"So why don't you come then?"

"I don't know." I glance over at him to discover he's smiling. "I guess I'm just lazy," I confess.

He laughs again. "Well, at least you're honest."

If he only knew.

"Does it bother you that I don't come on Sundays?" I ask as we go inside. "But that I'm willing to come work at the soup kitchen, I mean?"

"No, not at all. In fact, it just makes me really curious about you."

"How's that?"

"Well, most folks would rather come to church than work at the soup kitchen."

"Really?" I wait as he opens the door to the hallway that leads to the kitchen.

"You bet. So I guess I'm wondering what makes you do the opposite." He pauses now to really study me.

"I'm not sure. I guess I just feel more comfortable actually doing something that helps someone, you know? It feels better than getting dressed up to go sit on a pew and listen to someone just preach." I feel my eyes open wide now like I can't believe I just said that to a preacher. "Not that you don't do a good job up there, Pastor Leon, I don't mean—"

"Hey, it's okay, Zoë. I think I understand what you're saying." He nods as we reach the kitchen. "In fact, I think I'm in total agreement with you."

"You mean that I don't need to come to church?" I feel hopeful now. Like maybe I'm about to get his blessing to keep skipping out on church. Maybe I can even get him to call my parents or maybe send an excuse note home.

"Oh, no, I'm not saying you don't *need* to come to church," he says. "I'm just saying maybe you've got your priorities straight."

We're in the kitchen now and the other workers have stopped their usual chatter, like they want to hear what we're talking about. "What do you mean?" I ask in a quiet voice.

"Well," he says in a not-so-quiet voice. "God's Word says that true religion is to go out to visit poor widows and orphans without getting yourself defiled."

"But what does that mean?"

Now he smiles this really coy kind of smile, like he knows this really good secret, but he's not going to tell me. "I guess you'd have to come to Sunday worship service to find *that* out."

This makes the kitchen crew laugh, as if they get the joke and it's on me. But I don't really mind since I probably deserve it. And what he said is almost intriguing enough to make me want to come to church. Well, almost. Sleeping in on Sunday mornings still sounds pretty tempting to me.

"Here you go, Zoë," says Mavis Malheur, queen of the soup kitchen, as she hands me a potato peeler and nods to a mountain of potatoes over by the sink. "You know what to do, girl."

"Is this my punishment for not coming to church?" I ask over my shoulder, but Mavis just laughs.

"No, child, it's just that your young fingers can do it much faster than the rest of ours."

And so we all joke and laugh as I stand over the sink peeling potato after potato. And I think that if this was what church was like, it might not be so bad. Pastor Leon did get me to thinking a little. I do wonder what he meant about that visiting widows and orphans thing. It just sounds pretty weird to me. I mean I sort of get the widow and orphan part because I think a really good person would want to help people who are down and out. And isn't that kind of like the soup kitchen? But I don't get the "without getting defiled part." I mean what's up with that? I know that being defiled is like being really dirty, or worse. But besides getting all grungy and smelling like onions, how could helping in the soup kitchen possibly defile me? Very mysterious.

Soon it's time to serve the meal, and as usual, I am asked to go out to help. Now you'd think I would like this part of the job since putting food on plates is lots easier than peeling potatoes or washing dishes, but it always makes me a little uneasy. In fact, I usually try to get out of it.

"Are you sure you wouldn't rather have me start cleaning up back here?" I offer.

But Mavis just shakes her head. "No, Zoë," she says. "I think these hungry people would enjoy seeing your pretty, smiling face."

"You say that every time," I remind her.

"That's exactly right." She smiles. "So why do you even bother to ask me?"

I roll my eyes at her. "I just think you want to get rid of me so that you ladies can sneak back into the kitchen and put your feet up while I'm out there working," I tease.

"That's right. And we'll probably sample some of that apple cobbler while we're at it." Then she gives me a little push.

I go out and stand behind the big table that's full of big pots and aluminum trays of food. Even though they call it a soup kitchen, they rarely serve soup here. Today it's meat loaf, potatoes and gravy, and other things. I see the line of people and it looks longer than usual. They're waiting for Pastor Leon to welcome them in and then bless the food. I try not to look at them too closely. Their clothes are always pretty old and worn and often unwashed, but it's their eyes that tend to haunt me. They can't hide their sadness or hopelessness, and I can tell they're embarrassed by their poverty and wish they could be anywhere but here. It usually gets better after they get their food and sit down and begin eating. People begin to visit and lighten up, and Pastor Leon goes out of his way to make everyone feel comfortable. He often has someone perform music or some special kind of entertainment.

But it's always hardest at the beginning, as they first come into the room and approach the serving table. And this is when I usually find myself wanting to just stare down at the food.

Fortunately, I'm a pretty good actress. So once the people start coming up to me, I force a smile to my face and I say the things I think they might like to hear. Just shallow things like how cold it is today or how great this meat loaf is or whatever. But, believe me, it's *not* easy. The worst moment is when this girl who seems to be about my age walks up. The first thing I notice is this beautiful auburn hair that goes clear down her back in a long braid that's tied with a ratty-looking piece of yarn. But it's her expression that gets to me. She keeps her eyes downward and looks totally miserable about being here. And who can blame her? I mean how humiliating would it feel to be so desperate that you have to come to a church for free food? Even so, I try to think of something nice to say.

"I love your hair," I quickly say. This makes her look up and study me with what seems a bored or maybe unconvinced expression. "Really," I try again. "The color is so beautiful."

"Thanks," she mutters as she looks back down at her tray and moves through the line. But I watch her as she goes to find a seat. And I feel really bad for her. I mean not only is she eating at a soup kitchen, but the outfit she's wearing is so bad. She must've gotten it out of one of those free clothing boxes piled up in the back of the church. But, honestly, her fake-fur-trimmed ski jacket looks like something my grandma might've worn for one season then thrown out because it was so ugly. But I conceal these thoughts, keeping my sunny smile pasted across my plastic face. Believe me, I often leave here feeling more drained than after a two-hour performance where I'm starring in the lead role. I know it sounds weird, but it's the truth.

Finally, the serving is done, including seconds (which didn't last for long), and I am relieved to go back into the kitchen where I can begin cleaning up. But as soon as I start scrubbing a big pot, I hear some music starting to play, and I realize that it's really pretty good. It sounds like a live band and so after the pot is clean, I decide to stick my head out for a quick peek.

But I am shocked to see Nate Stein up there in the center of the little makeshift stage. He's singing and playing lead guitar, along with a few other guys who are playing bass, drums, and keyboard. I stand there in my dirty apron next to the kitchen door, just listening until the song ends, and then I enthusiastically clap along with everyone else. These guys are really good.

That's when Nate notices me and gives me a surprised little nod before he introduces his band and his next song. I listen a bit longer before I feel guilty about neglecting my work and return to the kitchen.

Just as the last tray of dishes is slid into the big industrial dishwasher, I hear Mavis calling me.

"Someone here to see you, Zoë," she says with this sly grin.

"Hey, Nate," I say as I wipe my hands on my apron and push a stray piece of hair from my eyes.

"What're you doing here, Zoë?"

I hold up my hands. "What's it look like?"

He laughs. "Who'da thought?"

"Your band sounds great," I tell him.

"Thanks, I've been promising Pastor Leon that we'd come play once we got our drummer replaced."

"You know Pastor Leon?"

"Sure, this is where I go to church."

I nod. "Oh."

"But I haven't gone here for that long." Then he kind of frowns. "Do you go here too?"

I give him a sheepish smile. "Oh, not so much. But my parents do."

"But you work in the soup kitchen?"

"Yeah. I'm told that's kind of weird."

"Actually, I think it's kind of cool."

We talk for a bit longer, but then his band buddies call for him to come and help them pack up.

"I better go," he says.

I nod. "Yeah, me too."

Then I go back and finish wiping down the counters, turn in my apron, and finally leave.

I feel kind of funny when I leave, like I'm wondering what I am really doing there. Not that those people don't make me feel at home, they totally do. And I really like Mavis. Okay, Pastor Leon too. Maybe I'm just questioning why it is that I'm not interested in going to church. Especially after hearing that Nate goes.

As I get into Mom's car, I remember that it hasn't always been like this. There was a time, back when I was about seven, that I actually liked going to church. But it only lasted about a year. Our Sunday school teacher was this sweet little lady named Mrs. Fieldstone. She was a great storyteller, and she always brought homemade treats and told us how much God loved us. She made Bible stories seem real. Come to think of it, it was in her Sunday school class that I invited Jesus into my heart. Or at least that's how I remember it. But that was nearly ten years ago and I'm not even sure if it was for real. Besides, I have a strong feeling that whatever I did back then has nothing to do with who I am now. In fact, I'm sure that's the way I want to keep it. I mean my life seems pretty okay to me. It's not like I'm doing anything that's really wrong.

I turn toward the mall and tell myself to stop thinking about such weird stuff as I search for a good parking spot. Even Pastor Leon said he wasn't trying to lay a guilt trip on me.

"Just forget about it," I tell myself as I lock Mom's car and hurry over to Banana Republic (where my gift certificate is for). Okay, I'm not that crazy about Banana Republic anymore (that was last year), but how can I expect my grandma to keep up with such things? Besides, as I'm sure she or Mom would tell me, you shouldn't look a gift horse in the mouth. Like I know what that's supposed to mean.

So I'm walking through Banana Republic in search of something totally amazing to wear to the party tonight, and I suddenly remember the girl I'd noticed at the soup kitchen today. I remember the look on her face—total hopelessness—and the pathetic-looking jacket she had on. Even so, I tell myself, at least the jacket's warm, right? And why am I thinking about this anyway?

But it won't go away. And as I'm walking through the perfectly arranged shelves and racks at Banana Republic, it's like I cannot stop obsessing over this poor girl and wondering about how miserable her life must be and how awful it must feel to be in her shoes (which were a nasty pair of old cheap tennis shoes).

And finally, these thoughts just totally spoil this whole shopping experience for me. Feeling upset and ridiculous, I hand the sweater I've just picked out back to the smooth-looking salesgirl.

"Do you need a different size?" she asks.

I just shake my head. "I need a different heart." Naturally, she looks at me like I'm totally crazy. Maybe I am.

So I leave Banana Republic and get into my mom's car and actually start crying. Now what's up with this? I mean really, my life's been going pretty well lately. I've got a good role in the school play. I'm dating a totally cool guy. What the crud is wrong with me?

I start the car and tell myself it's probably just PMS or maybe I need a good long nap. Whatever it is, I'm sure it will go away eventually. And so I go home and take a shower to remove all the soup kitchen crud then fall into my bed and sleep soundly. So soundly that I don't even wake up until after seven!

Now I'm totally frantic when I realize how late it is. Not only do I have *nothing* to wear tonight, I haven't even taken the time to call Emily about this whole Todd and Shawna thing. And now I've got to scramble just to come up with something halfway decent from my own closet before Justin gets here. Oh, how I wish Amy still lived at home at moments like this. She always had a closet worth raiding.

I finally manage to put together an outfit that's not too lame. In fact, as I look at my reflection in the full-length mirror, I'm thinking,

Not bad! I've never tried wearing these boots with this skirt before, but I must say, it looks pretty hot.

It's like ten minutes before eight and I think maybe I actually have time to call Emily, especially if Justin is running late. So I quickly dial her number, but her mom tells me that she's on a date with Todd.

"Tell her I called," I say in a disappointed voice.

"Is everything okay, Zoë?" her mom asks with her typical concern. Emily's mom is the sweetest.

"Oh, yeah, everything is great," I assure her. "I just need to talk to Emily about, uh, about *something*." I try to make my voice sound cheerful as I tell her goodbye.

But I really want to ask Mrs. Schuler where Emily and Todd went tonight, and then I want to go there myself, and I want to grab Emily and tell her that Todd's a total jerk and that she should dump him right now. But it's too late for that. At least for tonight. Poor Emily!

eight

JUSTIN AND I DON'T TALK MUCH AS HE DRIVES TO THE PARTY. I'M PROBA-
bly being quiet because I feel sort of guilty for lying to my mom.

"So what are you and Justin up to tonight?" she asked when I
came downstairs just a few minutes before he got there.

"We're going to a party," I tell her in an innocent-sounding
voice. Okay, that wasn't a lie, but the next part was. "It's a surprise
birthday party for this really good friend of his." I think I sounded
fairly convincing. "I haven't met the guy yet, but I guess he and
Justin have been friends since they were little kids."

"Oh, that sounds nice." But then my mom looked concerned.
"Shouldn't you take him something? I have some nice cards in my
desk if you want to—"

"That's okay, Mom," I said quickly. "Justin got something for
him that's supposed to be from both of us."

"Oh, good for him. That Justin seems like such a nice boy. So
thoughtful."

But he seems unusually "thoughtful" as he silently drives across
town. Suddenly I'm concerned that something might be wrong between
the two of us. "Everything okay?" I finally ask in a tentative voice.

"Huh?" He turns to look at me, almost as if he's forgotten that
I'm even here.

"You're being so quiet," I tell him. "I just wondered if every-thing was all right."

"Sorry. I guess I was just thinking."

"Are you worried about something?"

"Well, I suppose I'm a little worried about the SAT test next week, and whether or not I'll be accepted into the college that my dad seems determined I need to attend. Just stupid stuff like that."

"That's not stupid, Justin." I sigh as the reality hits me. "I guess I kind of forget that you're a senior sometimes. I suppose you have a lot to think about."

"Yeah." Then he seems to relax a little. "But I guess I don't have to think about *everything* right now."

"That's right." Then I reach over and gently massage the back of his neck. "Relax," I tell him. "Just give yourself a little break tonight."

"Sounds good to me."

The party's in an older, slightly run-down subdivision, and from the number of cars filling the driveway, as well as lining both sides of the street, I'm guessing there must be a lot of kids here. But as soon as we go inside and push our way through a hot and crowded front room where the music is blaring loudly, I begin to realize that I don't really recognize anyone.

Not only that, but I don't think this is just a "high school" party since, judging by conversations, a lot of the people here are in their twenties and older. But even more disturbing is the fact that not only is there alcohol being served (which I expected), but I can also smell marijuana smoke, and my guess is that there may be other things going on here too.

Now I don't like to come across as this uptight chick who can't cut loose occasionally, but I'm thinking this just isn't the kind of party that strikes me as fun. And I wonder what made Justin think it was a good idea to bring me here. Or what made him want to be here himself.

But he is already mixing a couple of drinks from the open bar and he turns around and hands one to me. "Bottoms up," he says with a grin.

"What is it?" I ask.

"Just a Brown Cow," he tells me as if I should know what that means.

"What's that?" I ask, feeling slightly stupid, but not really caring either.

"Rum and Coke." He holds up his glass. "Cheers!"

Well, I suppose one drink can't hurt me, and maybe if I bide my time for, say, fifteen or twenty minutes, I might be able to talk him into going someplace else. And so I do my best to drink what actually tastes like nail polish remover (or how I imagine it might taste) but, for his sake, I do pretend to like it. And, of course, this results in him mixing me another one. I'm about to refuse it when he's greeted by the guy who must be hosting this moronic party.

"Hey, Justin," this guy says as he slaps him on the back. "I'm glad you came. Whazzup, man?"

Then Justin introduces me to "Nick" and the two of them start talking like they really are the old buddies I'd described to my mom earlier. And then, just when I'm not paying attention, they both disappear. Like *poof!* they're gone.

Well, I walk around the crowded and sweltering house and discover that it's a lot larger than it looked from the outside. But I don't see Justin anywhere. And naturally, since I don't really know this Nick guy, I don't feel comfortable walking into rooms where the doors are closed. I mean who knows what I might discover?

I finally decide to give up when I notice a vacant easy chair in a somewhat quiet corner of the living room. So I sit down, cross my legs, fold my arms, and simply do some people watching. And let me tell you, there's some strange stuff going on here, and in a weird way it's kind of interesting. But I do begin to notice a pattern. It's like guys and girls don't really know each other, but they visit a little, pair off and dance for a bit, and then they just sort of split. I'm not sure if they're sick of the party and going somewhere else or what. I'm not even sure that I care. I just want to get out of this place myself.

And I'm pretty curious as to where Justin and Nick have disappeared to and when Justin plans to return. If my parents hadn't been planning on going to a movie tonight (and *if* it wasn't such a sleazy party), I would call my dad and beg him to pick me up. But I realize that's pretty childish.

So here I sit, just watching everyone. I figure there's not much else I can do. I sit here for about half an hour or more, I'm guessing, but I'm getting more and more irritated with Justin for abandoning me like this. And then this guy, who looks as if he could be like thirty-something, decides to perch on the arm of my chair like he has a right to. I mean what is wrong with people?

"How's it going?" As if it's any of his business.

I kind of shrug in hopes of appearing unfriendly then say, "Okay, I guess."

"Okay, you guess?" he echoes in a sympathetic tone. "That doesn't sound very good to me. What could possibly be troubling a pretty girl like you?"

I glance nervously over my shoulder, really wishing that Justin would reappear and get me out of this place. "I seem to have lost my boyfriend somewhere in here." I think this sounds like a fairly obvious hint, as in, *I have a boyfriend, so bug off.*

But he just laughs. "Well, maybe that's not such a problem." Then he holds out his hand. "I'm Mike, I happen to live here. Now what's your name?"

I'm at a total loss now, and so I simply tell him my name and hope that he'll decide I'm pretty boring and just blow. But this guy is stubborn.

"Can I refresh your drink?" he offers.

I notice that I have actually finished off my drink and I don't know whether to be concerned or proud. But thinking I might be able to lose this loser, I say, "Sure, but I'd really like just a plain Coke this time."

"No problem."

And for a few moments I am left in peace again. Well, in as much peace as this place can offer. I consider abandoning my spot before Mike returns, but it has a good vantage point for when Justin decides to make an appearance. I watch as couples go up and down the steps. And I begin to notice something else that seems kind of weird. It's like a lot of the girls are wearing these really odd colors of lip gloss. I mean seriously, in the past five minutes I've seen purple, blue, orange, yellow, even green. Like what's up with that?

Then Mike returns with my drink in hand. But now I'm slightly suspicious. "Is this *just* a Coke?" I ask.

He nods. "Just like the lady ordered."

Even so, I take a cautious sip. It wouldn't surprise me if he had spiked it with something stronger. But it actually tastes okay and it's cold and icy. But as I drink it, Mike remains perched on the arm of my chair like he owns the joint, which I suppose he does. But he's making small talk about the CD that's playing right now and how he saw this group in concert like ten years ago (I mean I would've been like seven back then!). I try not to encourage him with too many responses, although I do seem to be loosening up a bit. Maybe the alcohol has taken effect. And finally I can't help but mention the weird fashion statement that seems to be going on in this place.

"What's up with all the lip gloss?" I ask him. "I've never seen so many strange colors."

He laughs now. "Oh, that's for the rainbow room."

"The rainbow room?"

"Yeah," he tells me as he stands up and takes my hand. "You want to see it?"

"Sure," I tell him, but I notice that I'm feeling a little unsteady on my feet as I stand and I suddenly wonder if it's possible to get drunk on just two Brown Cows. But it's like the room is beginning to spin and I feel funny.

"Are you sure that was just a Coke?" I ask him as I hold up my empty glass. I seem to be working hard to form my words so they don't sound slurred.

He nods, but instead of one head, I think I see two. Then he is leading me down the stairs. I don't actually feel my feet on the steps, but I sense I am going down. Then he opens a door to another room where another sort of party seems to be going on. There are colored lights, but it's very dim and the music isn't quite as loud as upstairs. It looks like guys and girls are mingling around, dancing and drinking and making out. But it's all kind of blurry and out of focus. I try to blink and adjust my vision, but it's not helping.

"This is Zoë," I hear Mike telling someone.

"Hey, Zoë," says a blonde girl who seems to have two heads or maybe three. "Welcome to the rainbow room."

"Huh?" I feel seriously nauseated now.

"Here," she says, "let me help you."

Now I'm somewhat relieved. Like maybe someone understands my dilemma. "Thanks," I mutter. That's when I realize she's wiping something onto my mouth. I sputter and spit. "What's that?" I demand, stepping back.

She laughs. "Just lip gloss. You get to be *magenta* tonight."

"Huh?" I reach my hand to my mouth and touch the sticky substance she's just smeared onto my lips. "I don't *want* to be magenta," I mutter as I turn around and stagger to the door. "I *want* to go home."

But Mike is still holding on to my hand, telling me to just take it easy and relax. But that's when my stomach just totally flips over and the next thing I know I am violently barfing.

"Gross!" he yells as he shoves me away. I'm relieved to get away from him, but I still feel sick as I head for the door. I desperately want a bathroom. As I stagger down the hallway, hanging on to the wall for support, Justin grabs me by the arm. At least I think it's him. I blink my eyes since my vision is pretty blurry.

"Zoë!" he exclaims and then I know it's him. "Where have you been?"

"Where've I been?" I manage to echo in a slurred voice. "Whad'ya mean where've *I* been? Where've *you* been?"

Then he takes me by my shoulders and pulls me toward him so that he can see my face in the dimly lit hallway. "What on earth have you been doing?" he demands.

"Whad'ya think I've been—" Then I stop. "I need a bathroom, Justin, I'm going to barf again."

"*Again?*" But he doesn't waste time and fortunately, we are right next to one and he opens the door and I run in and just barely make it to the toilet in time. Finally I am done, and feeling a little better, although my head is still throbbing, I go to the sink, but when I look into the mirror I see those awful smudges of magenta across my mouth. I get some tissues and manage to wipe off the nasty lip gloss before I wash my face with soap and cold water. All the while, Justin is just sitting on a bench by the door silently watching me. By the time I finish, my hands are shaking and I am so upset that I'm crying.

That's when I turn and look at Justin. With tears streaming down my cheeks, I demand, "Why did you bring me here? And why did you leave me like that?"

"Nick was just showing me something." His eyes seem to avoid mine and suddenly I wonder if this guy is really who I thought he was.

"What was he showing you?" I ask with my hands on my hips. I feel like I'm returning to my old self now.

"This new video game," he says quickly. "I guess we just lost track of time." Then he steps up and takes me in his arms. "I'm sorry, Zoë."

Well, his sympathy is my complete undoing, and I totally break into sobs as he holds me. "It was awful," I blubber. "I was feeling sick and I couldn't find you. . . ." I continue to cry as I tell him about Mike and how he took me to the rainbow room.

"Mike took you to the rainbow room?"

I nod then wipe my running nose.

"Did, uh, well, did anything happen?"

I tell him about the lip gloss and how I threw up and then Justin pulls me toward him as he gently rubs my back. "I'm so sorry, Zoë," he says in a gentle voice. "Are you okay now?"

I pull away to reach for a fresh tissue. "I guess so," I tell him. "But I want to go home now."

"But it's not even ten."

"I don't care."

When I get home, I am relieved to see that my parents aren't back from their movie yet. As a result, I am able to slip up to my room without having to explain why I came home early.

But as I prepare for bed, I feel very disturbed. Not just by tonight, although that was certainly bad enough! But I'm also thinking about what I saw in the wardrobe room yesterday, and about all the stuff that girls like Thea and Kirsti like to talk about in the locker room, and I am seriously concerned about sex in general, like what is going on, and why people act like that. And furthermore — WHAT IS WRONG WITH THIS FREAKING PLANET???

nine

WITH A FUZZY TONGUE AND ACHING HEAD, I TIPTOE DOWNSTAIRS THE next morning in search of some orange juice. But it must be later than I think since my parents are already up. As usual, they invite me to go to church with them. I'm sure they don't expect me to go, but at least I have an honest excuse today.

"I feel kind of sick," I tell them as I pour a small glass of juice.

"What's wrong?" asks my mom, her brows drawn together in concern.

"I don't know," I say. "Maybe something I ate last night."

My dad puts down his coffee cup and narrows his eyes. "You kids weren't out drinking, were you?"

I make a face. "Yeah, sure, Dad, I got totally plastered. You bet." Then I attempt a smile. "If it's any comfort to you, I was in bed before ten o'clock last night."

"It might be the flu," says my mom. "It's going around, you know."

"Maybe so," I tell her. "I think I'll just lay low today."

I stay in bed for the rest of the morning but finally feel better around noon. And that's when Emily calls.

"Mom said to call you," she tells me.

"Yeah, I wanted to talk to you about . . . something."

"Something?"

"Yeah, but I'd rather talk face-to-face."

"Want to go to the mall?" she asks.

And so it's agreed that she'll pick me up in half an hour. I still feel kind of sluggish as I get dressed. I try not to think about what it is I want to tell her or how I will say it.

But soon we are on our way and she demands that I tell her what's wrong.

"Well, something happened on Friday," I begin slowly. "It was at play practice and, well, it's kind of hard to tell you this, but I think you have the right to know." And so I continue, stumbling and bumbling along until I've finally told her the whole story of Todd and Shawna in the wardrobe room.

Her lips are pressed tightly together as she parks her car in the mall parking lot. "That's disgusting, Zoë."

"Yeah," I say in my best "duh" voice. "I *know* that, Emily. It's not like I enjoy telling you."

"Well, it's also pretty unbelievable. I mean Todd and I were together on Friday night and last night. And, if anything, he seems more in love with me than ever. I can't believe he'd do something like that."

"But I saw it—"

"You say you were only in the room for a couple of seconds?"

"Well, yes."

"And it was dark in there?"

"I turned on the lights."

"And you're absolutely positive it was Todd and Shawna?"

I consider this. "Well, I was kind of in shock, but, yes, I'm positive it was Todd and Shawna."

"I just can't believe this, Zoë." She turns and stares at me now. "I mean you only saw them for a few seconds, you said you were in shock, and you even said you couldn't see Shawna's face. Are you absolutely certain about this? Could you swear it in a court of law?"

Now I begin questioning myself. I mean with all the crazy things that have happened lately, and still feeling kind of groggy, suddenly I'm not too sure about anything.

"Are you, Zoë?" She's holding onto my arm now, squeezing it pretty tightly.

I shake my head and sigh. "Oh, I don't know, Emily. I mean I think I'm sure, but it's all kind of hazy now. Maybe this wasn't the best time to talk about all this." Then I tell her about what happened last night and she is totally appalled.

"You're kidding?"

"Why would I joke about something like that?"

Emily's eyes are wide now. "Do you *know* what a rainbow party is?"

"I didn't say rainbow party," I correct her. "I said they called it the 'rainbow room.'"

"And they put magenta lip gloss on you?"

"Yeah, what's up with that?"

Then, acting like Miss Know-It-All, Emily tells me that a rainbow party is when girls put on all different colors of lip gloss (like red, purple, pink, blue, orange) and then take turns applying these colors onto a certain private part of a guy's anatomy until he has a "rainbow" assortment of colors.

"EWW! THAT IS TOTALLY DISGUSTING!" I practically scream at her. "That is so sick, Emily! I can't believe you even know—"

"Hey, don't yell at me. It's not like I make this stuff up myself."

"Where did you hear that?"

"I don't know. Probably Thea or Kirsti."

"Do they do that? I mean in groups like that?"

She shrugs now. "Who knows? But I sort of doubt it. I mean they may be into some skanky stuff, but I don't think they'd sink that low. Really, I have a feeling that only seriously lame girls would do something that disgusting. I mean some girls would do anything to get a guy to like them." Now she looks at me like maybe I fall into this seriously lame and desperate category.

"What are you saying?" I demand.

"I don't know." She shrugs. "If the shoe fits—"

"Emily Schuler!" I yell. "I can't believe you think that I'd—"

"Hey, you just told me you were there, Zoë."

"Not willingly!"

"Well . . ."

Suddenly the idea of walking around the mall with my so-called best friend sounds very unappealing to me.

"Like I already told you," I begin in what I hope is a calm and controlled voice, "Justin gave me two drinks before he vanished, then this Mike dude moved in and tried to take advantage."

Her eyebrows rise slightly. Almost like she doesn't completely believe me. "Yeah, whatever."

Well, now I am seriously fried. "Yeah, whatever!" I yell as I open the door. "I don't think I feel like doing the mall today," I snap as I get out of her car.

"Hey, Zoë, you don't have to come all unglued." She quickly gets out too. "I can't help it if your story sounds a little far-fetched."

I hold up my hands. "Just forget it, Emily. I'm going home."

"Don't you need a ride?"

But I'm already walking toward the bus stop. "No."

"But, Zoë!"

Without looking back, I yell, "Just forget about it, Emily."

I feel tears streaking down my cheeks as I march toward the bus stop. I mean Emily and I have been best friends since middle school. We've always been loyal to each other. Oh, sure, we've had little disagreements before, but never anything like this. I can't believe that she thinks I would've willingly gotten myself into a situation like that. And the fact that she knows what a rainbow party is but never even told me — well, what kind of a friend is she, anyway? And what about the fact that she didn't even believe me about Todd and Shawna? Like I would lie to her? Well, maybe it is time for Emily and me to part ways. I mean who needs friends like that anyway?

I finally stop crying by the time the right bus arrives. But as I sit there and look out the steamy window I feel confused. Totally confused. I honestly try to see this thing from Emily's point of view. Okay, maybe she truly believes that Todd wouldn't do something like that. But does she really think I would make it up? No, she just questioned whether I really saw what I am sure I saw. I suppose she could just be in denial. But why wouldn't she trust me, her best friend?

Finally, I decide that this is probably what happens when guys enter the picture. It's like we melt down and our brains turn to mush and we start thinking and acting like crazy women. Or not. I guess I'm not sure about much of anything anymore. I feel kind of lost today, like maybe I need a compass or something to help me find my way home. Even when the bus drops me off at the stop that I think is closest to my house, I still feel disoriented. I know this is partially due to the fact that I haven't ridden this bus since I was in middle school. But somehow, everything feels different. I feel different. And suddenly I actually wish I was just thirteen again. I wish that it was just Emily and me riding the bus to the mall to shop for a new T-shirt or pair of flip-flops, and that our only use for boys was to flirt a little and then make fun of them when they didn't seem to get it. But times have changed. And so have I.

I finally get my bearings straight and decide that I need to turn left down Taylor Street. And somehow I manage to find my way home. And when I get there, my mom tells me that Justin brought flowers by, and that he was concerned about me getting sick last night.

"He really is a thoughtful young man," she says as she shows me a vase of red roses.

"Wow," I say as I smell the fragrant blooms. "No one ever sent me flowers before."

Then she got a little more serious. "You know what red roses mean, don't you?"

Feeling ignorant for the second time today, I just shake my head. "Not really."

"True love." Then she winks at me.

"Oh."

"But don't let it go to your head, Zoë."

I roll my eyes at her. "Don't worry."

Justin calls later to ask how I'm doing and if I liked my flowers.

"I feel better," I tell him. "And the roses are beautiful. But I guess I'm still a little bummed."

"Why?"

I sigh. "Oh, I don't know. That stuff last night was kind of upsetting. But today Emily and I got into a big fight and it got kind of ugly."

"You told her about Todd and Shawna?" His voice sounds shocked.

"Yeah. I mean she's my best friend." I hear the defensiveness in my voice. "And I'd want her to do the same for me if I were in her place."

"Oh-oh," he says. "Guess I better watch my step."

I try to laugh but am actually wondering if this might be a real possibility. I mean if someone who comes across as devoted as Todd can cheat on his girlfriend, then why should I think that I'm safe?

But of course I don't say this. I look at the roses, now sitting in the middle of my bureau, and smile. "Sorry," I tell him. "I don't want to start sounding like a guy-basher."

He laughs. "Don't worry. I'd understand if you did. That party last night was really over the top. I never would've taken you there if I'd known what was going on."

I sigh now, reassuring myself that Justin really is the guy I believe him to be. We talk for a while longer then Justin tells me that he needs to study for SATs, and I realize I still have some homework, so we hang up.

As usual (I have a hard time studying without background noise), I turn on the small TV in my room as I read my English lit assignment. But before long, my lit book is flopped facedown in my lap and I am tightly focused on the premier movie that's been playing for about half an hour now. It's one of those hot and steamy movies where everyone is cheating on everyone and the heroine can't make up her mind about which guy she loves the most, but I am amazed at how many sex scenes are in it. Why am I paying so much attention to the sex scenes? I suppose it's because of all that's been going on lately. I guess I'm just trying to figure this whole thing out. Like what's okay to do? What's not? And where does a girl go for advice in these matters anyway?

And so, just for fun, I decide to keep track of how many sex scenes are in this movie. I actually make little slashes on my notebook to keep count. Now I know this sounds slightly whacked out, and I'd never admit this stupid little activity to anyone, but it's actually kind of interesting. And while I'm at it, I decide to see how many commercials have sexual undertones in them as well.

By the time the credits roll at eleven o'clock, I am stunned by the number.

So I'm asking myself, is this why our culture is so obsessed with sex right now? Or has it always been this way? And are the things I'm seeing on TV (things we all know took place in the White House) acceptable? I mean this TV movie is one thing, but I happen to know that MTV and other channels are much, much worse.

And I'm wondering, are there any rules about sexual things? And if so, who makes them anyway? And do they change? And if we play by the "rules," will we be spared from getting hurt? Or maybe everyone who plays gets hurt. Finally, my brain just can't take it anymore. It's all so confusing and I know that I need to tune it out before I go flipping nuts.

And so I tell myself to go to sleep. But it seems like I toss and turn for hours, and even when I finally go to sleep my dreams are riddled with sexual confusion. When I wake up the next morning I feel more mixed up than ever. Can't someone give me some directions, or maybe just a sexual compass so I'll know which way to go?

ten

I HAVE AVOIDED SHAWNA ALL DAY. AND FINALLY SHE CONFRONTS ME WHILE I'm on my way to play practice.

"What's up with you?" she asks in a grumpy voice.

I just shrug. "Nothing."

"Come on, Zoë. I thought we were friends."

So I turn and look at her with narrowed eyes. "Yeah, I *thought* we were friends too, Shawna. But friends don't cheat with their friends' boyfriends."

"I've never cheated on you," she tells me in a defensive tone.

"No, I mean my best friend's boyfriend." Actually, I should say my "ex-best friend" but that's beside the point.

"Oh." She looks down now, and I know that I've nailed her.

"Didn't Todd tell you that I walked in on you guys?"

Still looking down, she just shakes her head.

"Well, I did. And it was pretty shocking, not to mention disappointing."

"I'm sorry," she says in a small voice.

Suddenly I feel kind of bad for grilling her like this. Like who am I to go picking on others? "Yeah, I'm sorry too, Shawna. And maybe it's not fair to be mad at you, but I just think it was wrong. Really wrong."

She looks up and nods. "Yeah, it was wrong."

"Then why?" I peer into her eyes. "Why did you do it?" Now, I can't bring myself to admit that this is a double question. I mean first of all, I want to know why she cheated on Emily after I asked her not to. But next I want to know why she'd want to do *that* at all? I mean it seems disgusting and degrading to me. What's the payoff anyway?

"It was Todd's idea," she says in a quiet voice. "We were joking around, and it was kind of a dare, you know, and I suppose I thought I was being cool."

"Cool?" I can't contain myself now. "You think *that's* cool?"

She looks embarrassed now. "No, not really. I guess it seemed kind of daring. I don't know."

"Have you done that before?"

She shakes her head no.

So, I pull her off to the back of the auditorium where we can sit and talk without being overheard. "So what would make you want to do it then, Shawna?"

She shrugs. "I don't know."

"Doesn't it make you feel totally degraded? Like you're just this mindless sexual object?"

"I really like Todd."

"Did you think it would make him really like you? Did you honestly think it would make him break up with Emily?"

"He said that he was getting tired of her. He thinks she's boring."

"That's not what he tells Emily."

She frowns now. I can tell she's hurt.

"Can't you see he's just using you, Shawna? Doesn't that make you feel like a tramp?"

It almost looks like she's about to cry now.

"Look, I'm not trying to come down on you. The truth is, I'm trying to figure this thing out for myself. I mean it's kind of confusing."

She looks up with interest now. "What do you mean?"

And so I launch into what happened to me on Saturday night, sparing no details, and I wait for her reaction.

"Guys can be such scum," she finally says.

"But they can't very well do what they do without girls consenting." I'm thinking I sound a little bit like Casey now. But maybe I don't care.

She rolls her eyes now. "Don't be so sure, Zoë. I mean think about it. That guy at the party wanted to push you into something you didn't want to do. Believe me, I've had guys do stuff to me without my consent. Haven't you ever heard of date rape? Or do you really live under a stone?"

"Yeah, sure," I say quickly. "I saw a news show on it once. There was this university where—"

"It doesn't just happen in college. Trust me, Zoë, it happens all the time. Probably among your own friends."

"How do you know?"

"It's happened to me." But she says this in a hard voice, like it doesn't really matter. "But do you think that girls like me tell anyone about it?"

I study her then finally say, "Probably not."

"You're right. What good would it do for me to tell? I'd just end up looking like a total tramp while the guy gets off with a slap on the hand."

"That's not fair."

"When it comes to sex, nothing is fair, Zoë."

"That just seems all wrong."

"Tell me about it."

"Well, okay, Shawna." I try to reason with her. "If you really feel like that, then why did you have sex with Todd?"

She laughs now. "That's *not* sex."

"Huh?"

"You're still a virgin, right?"

I nod and feel like I'm about five years old.

"Well, you don't get it, do you?"

I sigh, knowing I'm over my head again. Mostly I'd like for this conversation to just end. I glance up to the stage, hoping that it's time for us to go up, but Mr. Roberts doesn't seem to be here yet.

"Look, you're not stupid, Zoë. You know what intercourse is, right?"

I roll my eyes. "Yeah, of course."

"Well, intercourse is sex. Outercourse is *not*."

"Outercourse?"

"Yeah, call it what you want, you know what I mean."

"*That's* not sex?"

"No, that's not."

"Well, I just don't get that."

"Don't you remember what President Clinton said about it?"

"I don't think I was paying attention."

Shawna laughs. "Yeah, that figures. But trust me, that's not sex."

I just shake my head. "Well, that just doesn't make any sense."

Now she laughs even louder. "It's the way it is, Zoë. Get used to it."

Get used to it? Yeah, you bet. I feel more confused than ever now. But Miss Lynnwood is calling everyone to the stage and it's time to end this stupid conversation.

"Are we okay, Zoë?" she asks with hopeful eyes.

"I guess so," I tell her as we walk toward the front. "The truth is that Emily and I aren't even speaking now. So whatever you do or don't do with Todd isn't any of my business."

She smiles with relief. "Really, Zoë, Todd told me that he plans to break up with her this week."

I seriously doubt this. I think Todd is just looking to get everything he can. But, like I told her, I plan to scoot on out of this messy little love triangle. It's really *not* my business. And the fact is, I have enough trouble trying to understand my own sexuality without trying to figure out everyone else's.

Midway through play practice I get to take a break and I sit down in the front row directly below the stage. I watch as Justin practices a lively song-and-dance scene. He's surprisingly good and I'm amazed at how easily he can pull off the corny lines and actually breathe a little life into them.

"He's good," says Nate as he sits down beside me.

"That's what I was just thinking."

"So, how's it going?"

I consider this. "I'm not really sure."

"Did you talk to Emily?"

"Huh?" I stare at him like he's from another planet. "What are you talking about?"

He looks slightly embarrassed now. "Casey told me."

"Casey told *you*?" I am totally stunned.

"She asked me to pray for you. Sorry, maybe I shouldn't have said anything."

"Why should this surprise me?" I say. "I mean it's not like anyone has secrets in this school."

"Not for long anyway."

"Did Casey tell you *everything*?"

He nods. "I feel sorry for Emily."

I sigh loudly. I'm not sure whether to be angry or embarrassed or to just let it go. But in some ways I'd like someone other than Emily and Shawna to talk to. "Yeah, she doesn't even believe me."

"That's too bad. But you told her the truth because you care about her. Right?"

"Yeah. But the whole thing still went south on me."

"Well, it's not over yet."

"What do you mean?"

"I mean you and Emily are good friends, and time may change how she sees this thing between you guys."

"You really think so?"

"Yeah."

"What makes you so smart about girl stuff?"

He laughs. "I don't know. I guess it's just a gut feeling."

"Well, you might be right, but I don't plan on telling Emily anything about Todd again. She can figure it out for herself."

He nods. "So, other than Emily, how're you doing, Zoë?"

I turn to look at him now, wondering why he's so interested in what's going on with me. "Why do you want to know?" I sound snippy even to myself. Maybe I'm just in a bad mood today.

He looks slightly offended, but just says, "Hey, I thought we were friends."

"Yeah, we are." I sigh. "I guess I'm just feeling defensive since my life seems a little confused right now."

"Confused?"

I shrug. "Just the regular stuff, you know."

He nods. "Oh yeah, I know."

I study him carefully, skeptical as to whether he could *possibly* know. How could someone like Nate understand all the crazy questions tumbling through my mind?

He laughs. "I know, you're thinking I wouldn't get it, right?"

"Yeah. Sort of."

"And you probably assume that since I'm a Christian, I wouldn't have the same kinds of problems as you, right?"

"Yeah, I guess so." I glance up to where Casey Renwick is playing Aunt Eller and cutting up with Justin. "I mean I know that Casey doesn't get it."

He laughs now. "You mean because she seems to have it all nailed down about things like dating and sex?"

"You got that right."

"Well, just because we're Christians doesn't mean that we have it all together, Zoë. But at least we have some help."

"Help?" I study him carefully.

"Yeah. God doesn't just tell us to obey him then set us out to sea to fend for ourselves."

"What kind of help does God give you?"

Nate considers this. "Well, for starters, he stays in a relationship with me so that he can guide me through sticky situations."

"Kind of like a body guard?"

He smiles and I notice, not for the first time, that he really has an attractive smile. "Not exactly," he says. "More like a little voice that reminds me about what's right and wrong."

"Right and wrong with Jiminy Cricket." I sigh. "Is life really that simple?"

"With God it's pretty straightforward. But don't get me wrong, Zoë, that doesn't mean it's always easy. Take me for instance. I can be in a situation where I know what's right. It can be simple and clear. But then I still have to choose to *do* right. And sometimes that's tough."

I sort of understand, but not completely. "It sounds good," I tell him, "but it doesn't make complete sense."

"Yeah," he agrees, "it never does. Not until you come to God yourself."

"Are you hinting at something?" I ask. "Are you trying to convince me to get down on my knees and invite God into my heart?" I can hear the sarcastic tone in my voice and I feel a little embarrassed, but I continue. "Will Pastor Leon give you a gold star if you lead me to God, Nate?"

But he's not offended. Or if he is, he sure doesn't show it. He just laughs. "Hey, I can't lead anyone to God, Zoë. God has to do that himself."

"Sorry," I say. "I didn't mean to sound so jaded. But I'm confused about so many things at the moment, I don't see how throwing religion into the puddle is going to help clear anything up."

"You might be surprised," he says. "Although I'm not talking about religion. I'm talking about a relationship with God. He made you and understands you and knows what you need to have a good life."

A *good* life? Now I wonder what that would be exactly. Or what it would feel like? Or if it's even possible. "Is that what you have, Nate?" I ask. "Do you have a good life?"

He chuckles. "Well, it's not perfect, that's for sure. But it's pretty good. I'm not complaining."

"Well, I'm not complaining either," I assure him as Justin jumps down from the stage then wipes off his brow with a hand towel.

"I'm plumb tuckered out," he says in his Oklahoma drawl then flops down in the seat beside me. "How'd that scene look from down here?"

"Fantastic," I tell him. "You were totally awesome."

"Yeah, you were really great," agrees Nate. "Your timing is perfect."

Justin studies Nate for a moment, almost like he wants to know what the two of us were just talking about, but he doesn't ask. "Timing is everything," he finally says in what almost sounds like a superior tone. I wonder if it's meant to be some sort of put-down to Nate. Then Justin slips his arm around me in what feels like a slightly possessive move. And to my surprise I want to pull away from him. But I don't.

"That's true," says Nate. "As long as you have your clock set right."

"Huh?" Justin frowns as I suppress laughter.

Then it's time for Nate and me to get ready for our next scene. Nate gives me a hand to help me up onto the stage and to my surprise I find myself mentally comparing these two guys. And here's what's weird: Today I'm not totally sure who scores higher.

eleven

As the week progresses, Emily continues to ignore me. And I continue to pretend that I don't care. Naturally, this puts me a little on the outside of my closest friends. Even Andrea, who is usually pretty nice, has been treating me like I've got cooties or something. And girls like Thea and Kirsti can be really blunt and almost cruel.

"What's up with you two?" Thea asks me as we're getting dressed after PE.

"Huh?" I try to act dumb.

"You and Emily," she probes. "You guys are acting like you hate each other. What happened? Did you make a move on Todd during play practice or something?"

I glance over at Shawna, who is silently tying her shoes, then I just roll my eyes at Thea and say, "Yeah, sure. I wait until Justin's not looking then Todd and I slip backstage and rip each others' clothes off."

Fortunately this makes them laugh. Well, except for Emily, who is scowling more than ever right now. Shawna has already slipped out without even being noticed. I suspect I may have offended her, but I'm not even sure that I care. More and more I'm thinking it's every man (or girl) for himself. Only the strong survive.

But, as a result of being snubbed by Emily, I've probably been hanging on to Justin more than ever. It's like he's become my social security blanket. Oh, I'm not saying that I only like him because of his status at Hamilton High. But sometimes I wonder if I'd be as attracted to him if he wasn't so popular.

In his defense, he has been sweeter than ever this week. I think he was actually feeling jealous of my friendship with Nate, and so it's like he's been trying to make sure that I know he and I are really a couple. Consequently I've made sure to cool things down with Nate. Other than our scenes together, I've managed to pretty much avoid him. But I must admit that I miss our little discussions. One thing about Nate is that you can trust him to say what he really thinks. He's not a hypocrite and he doesn't play games.

"Come here, Zoë," whispers Justin after we finish a scene and I know that a break is coming. He grabs my hand and pulls me with him to a corner that we recently discovered backstage. It's become a regular thing for us to meet there. We act like we're being really sneaky, like no one knows what we're up to (although I suspect that everyone does) then we enjoy a nice make-out session until we are either discovered or it's time to get back to rehearsal.

Now, I'm not saying that I don't enjoy kissing Justin, because, believe me, I do! Oh, I really do. But I've noticed how these little sessions are getting hotter and hotter, and I can tell it's only a matter of time before Justin will expect me to go all the way with him. And I'm just not sure that I'm comfortable with that. I mean despite all my whining and complaining about being the last virgin on the planet, I'm not absolutely positively sure that I'm ready to give that up yet.

Okay, I guess I'm mostly ready. And there are moments when I feel really ready—like when my heart's racing and I can barely breathe and lots of other new feelings are rushing through me like electricity. And I actually wonder if this is the real thing. Like, am I really in love? Or am I just a ticking time bomb of raging hormones and chemistry?

And then I wonder if it even matters, like, hey, maybe I should just jump in and get this milestone over with. At least I wouldn't be a liar anymore since all of my friends (except Shawna) think I'm not a virgin anymore anyway.

But there's this little bit of reservation going on inside of me, like this big question mark, and it makes me wonder if I'll regret giving in to Justin. I guess I'm just feeling confused and frustrated. Like, here's my big chance, but now I'm not so sure I want it. Or more than that, I'm not so sure it's the right thing for me to do. I really wish there was someone I could talk to about it. I mean this is a time when a girl really needs her best friend to be there for her. I remember how I used to listen to Emily going on and on about whether or not she'd do it with Todd (which is all water under the bridge now anyway), but I was there for her. Now when I need her, she's just leaving me high and dry.

Finally I decide to talk to Shawna. I mean she may not have exactly the same moral values as Emily, but at least she's experienced and should know what she's talking about. So on Thursday, I ask Shawna if she can give me a ride home and maybe stop for a bite to eat (so we can talk). Naturally, Justin is a little put out by this, but when I tell him that I just need to "talk to a woman" his eyebrows kind of lift up hopefully and he says, "Hey, that's cool."

"What's up?" asks Shawna when we finally sit down to our cheeseburgers, fries, and shakes. It's great how we can consume like thousands of calories without the slightest concern while we're working so hard on the play.

"I just needed to talk to someone," I tell her.

"About what?"

I take a sip of my shake as I consider beating around the bush then remember this is Shawna. "Sex," I state in a no-big-deal tone of voice.

She laughs. "Well, go for it."

So I explain how I'm feeling, how I really like Justin, but how I'm not really sure that it's right, but how maybe I should just get it over with.

She shrugs. "Yeah, that's pretty much how I felt."

"You mean the first time you did it?"

She nods.

"When was that?" I ask.

"I was fourteen."

"Fourteen?" I feel my eyes widen and hope I don't look too shocked.

"Yeah, looking back, I guess it was a little young. But at the time it seemed okay."

"And you really *wanted* to do it?"

She shrugs again. "I don't know."

"Were you pressured?"

She laughs now. "Ya think?"

"I don't know."

"Look, Zoë, the guy was seventeen. I was fourteen. Whose idea do you think it really was to get it on?"

I nod. "Well, did you enjoy it?"

Now she laughs even harder, but the sadness in her eyes betrays her. "I don't know any girl who really enjoys it. At least not the first time," she finally says.

I frown.

"Look, do you want me to be really honest with you, Zoë? Or

do you want the sugarcoated crud that girls like Thea and Kirsti dish out all the time?"

"Honesty would be nice."

So she launches into some fairly graphic details about how it's painful, awkward, humiliating, and best to just get it over with. "It's not like you see in the movies," she tells me as she dips a fry in ketchup.

"Oh."

"But don't worry," she assures me, "it gets better in time."

"It must," I say in a flat tone. "Otherwise people wouldn't keep doing it, right?"

Now she laughs so loudly that half the people in Dairy Queen are looking our way. "Yeah, and then everyone would stop reproducing and the human race would die off and before long apes would rule the planet."

I smile. "We probably don't need to worry about that."

"No, probably not."

I appreciate her candidness, but I'm not sure that it makes me any less confused. Finally I ask her the question that's really burning on my mind. "Shawna," I say just as we're finishing up, "if you had it all to do over again, would you have done anything differently?"

She looks down at the burger debris spread across our table and sighs. "Maybe."

"Like how?" I persist.

Now she looks slightly irritated, like maybe I've pushed her just a little too far, but she answers. "Like maybe I would've waited." Then she narrows her eyes and reaches for her bag. "But that's all I'm saying about that."

"Yeah, okay." We both stand up.

"Look, Zoë," she says as we exit the restaurant. "I'm not really an expert on this stuff. Maybe you should talk to someone else."

"Oh, I appreciate your honesty." I don't tell her that compared to girls like me or Emily or even Andrea, she is quite the expert. I have a feeling she would take that all wrong. So I change the subject as she drives me home.

Mom's the only one home when I get there. She's making a pot of tea in the kitchen and asks me if I'd like some. I'm not really big into tea, but think maybe this is an opportunity to talk to her. Not that I really want to ask her about sex exactly. I mean she's already given me the old mandatory sex talk (like back when I was twelve), and I could tell it made her uncomfortable then, but now that I'm older, maybe she's more relaxed. Still, I'm not sure. But I accept a cup of tea and we both sit down across from each other at the breakfast bar.

"How's the play coming?" she asks. Standard parental icebreaker question. And just to be nice I play along.

"It's okay."

"How's Justin doing?" Another standard question. Only this one means, *What's happening with you and Justin? Anything you'd like to talk to me about?* I can read this woman like a book.

"He's okay," I say. Now I feel a little guilty for my lack of cooperation. I mean here I am, the one who really needs to talk, and I'm just shutting her down right and left.

"Oh."

Then there's this long silence and I can tell it's up to me. "Mom?" I begin.

She looks up from the magazine she's been flipping through. "Yes?"

"Well, I'm trying to figure some things out. . . ."

"Like what, Zoë?"

"Oh, you know," I try to act nonchalant. "The old questions about life and love and happiness."

She kind of smiles. "Oh, all that simple stuff."

"What was it like when you met Dad?" I ask. "And I don't mean the standard story about how you met as short-term missionary volunteers in Peru then got married after only knowing each other for a month."

"What do you mean?"

"I mean what was it *really* like? How did you feel? How did you know you were really in love? How could you be so certain that he was the man you wanted to marry?" Naturally, I don't say "have sex with," since this is my mom, but I suppose this is what I'm really getting at. And in their case, if they're telling the truth, sex and marriage had pretty much come in hand in hand. So I think it works.

She pushes her magazine aside and considers this. "That's a lot of questions."

I nod. "Well, just do your best."

She smiles then launches into the story of how they met. They were both teachers in the mission school, she had just arrived to teach second grade, and he'd been there for about a year teaching high school science classes.

"It seemed like love at first sight," she says in a slightly dreamy voice (I prepare myself for doves and violins now). "I'd only been there a week and on Saturday, I'd gone to get produce at the market, you know where the locals set up tables and sell food outside, and I was so excited about all the fresh fruits and vegetables that I got carried away. I filled my burlap shopping bag so full that it split open—"

"Yeah, Mom, I know this part. And Dad helped you get your stuff home and all that. But what happened between the two of you, how did you feel? How did you know?"

"Right." She thinks for a moment. "Well, I noticed him right away. And I thought he was very handsome. You know, he still had a full head of hair back then, as well as a nice beard. But there was something in his eyes that just got to me, sort of took my breath away. . . ."

"Yeah?"

"And I remember when we got to my house, how he handed me back my melons and vegetables, well, his hand brushed mine a couple of times, and it felt like a little jolt of electricity. I think he must've felt it too, because we both looked at each other—right in the eyes—and, well, I think we both sort of knew that something was going on."

"So you had chemistry?"

She laughs. "Yes, you could definitely say that."

"What then?"

"He arranged for some friends to invite us both to dinner. The couple knew that he was interested in me and gave us plenty of time to be alone."

"And what did you do?" I tried not to imagine my parents kissing and pawing each other the way that Justin and I had done during play practice today.

"We just talked."

"Talked?" I feel disappointed. "That's all?"

"It was more than enough, Zoë. We just talked and talked and it's like we never had enough time to talk about everything."

"But what about the chemistry?"

"Oh, it was there. You could just about feel the electricity snapping in the air between us."

"But you just talked?" I can hear the skepticism growing in my voice.

"I can't explain it," she says. "But all we wanted to do was to get to know each other better."

"And you didn't kiss or anything?"

She laughs. "Of course we kissed. But not for a while."

"Why not?"

"Well, for one thing we were there as missionaries and we had to watch our manners. But, besides that, I think we both just wanted to get to know each other without being distracted with all the physical . . . well, pleasures." She smiles now, as if she's remembering something special. "But we knew it was there . . . we knew that we'd get the whole enchilada in time."

"So when did you first kiss?"

"We'd spent every spare moment together for about two weeks," she tells me. "And then your dad invited me to drive to a nearby town with him for dinner." She sighs now. "It was a beautiful evening, like something right out of a movie. Driving through the mountains as the sun set, eating at this place with little tables and strings of colored lights and candles at each table. So romantic. After dinner, we took a little walk and went across a bridge and then stopped and looked at the stars. And then your dad asked if he could kiss me."

"He actually *asked*?"

She nods. "Of course, I said yes. And what a kiss!"

"Okay, okay." I hold my hands now. "You don't have to go into all the details."

"You're the one who asked."

"Right. So, you guys kissed and then what?"

"Well, it was obvious that we were both highly attracted to each other. But we knew that we couldn't go around kissing each other back on the mission base. After just one more week, and only three weeks since we'd first met, your dad proposed."

"And you accepted."

"And we got permission from the mission director to elope," she says. "It worked out nicely since there was a one-week break the following week and we were able to enjoy a short honeymoon on the coast." She gets quiet now as if she's gone back in time. I don't know what to say. Then she continues. "Another interesting thing about our romance," she says in a serious voice, "we were both virgins, Zoë."

Now I'm holding up both hands, as in too much information. "That's okay, Mom," I say quickly. "We don't need to go there."

"But I want to. I want you to know that it was the best thing for both of us. We both came into the marriage completely free of some of the baggage that I see other people dealing with. Being married isn't easy for anyone, but it's so much better when you wait."

"Okay, okay." I nod. "I get the message. No regrets about waiting." Now I want to take this another direction. Any direction. "So did you have any regrets about anything?"

She nods now and suddenly I'm very curious.

"What?" I demand. "What did you regret?"

"Oh, sometimes I wish we'd been able to have a traditional wedding with our family and friends. But we would've had to wait a year for that. So it just didn't seem practical."

"But you didn't regret getting married so soon?"

"Not at all, Zoë. I knew, deep down in my heart that your dad was the one for me. I think God gave me a strong sense of peace about him. And I knew that I could trust him with my life. And, mostly, he hasn't let me down."

"Mostly?"

"Well, he's certainly not perfect. No one is. And you know as well as anyone that we've had our ups and downs. But, honestly, if I had it all to do over, I wouldn't change a thing. I would still marry your dad."

I pat her hand now. "That's nice, Mom. Thanks for telling me." Okay, it's still kind of a storybook romance, but if that's the way she really sees it, well, who am I to question it? I suppose things like that can happen to some people. Then I think of something else. "But were there any other guys, Mom? I mean before Dad?"

She looks kind of embarrassed now. "You mean boyfriends?"

I nod eagerly.

"Well, of course."

"Anything serious?"

"I don't know . . ."

But I can tell she *does* know. "Come on, Mom. Tell me."

"Okay." She looks up at the ceiling as if she's trying to remember, but I suspect it's a cover-up. I think she remembers it vividly. "There was Michael Stuart during my junior year."

"Yeah?" I lean forward with interest.

"We went together for most of the year, and I suppose I *thought* I was in love."

"Were you?"

She shrugs. "In retrospect? Probably not. But at the time I thought I was."

"What happened?"

"Nothing too unusual. Michael was a senior that year. He graduated and went to college. We wrote for a while. Then he met another girl and sort of broke my heart. But I got over it pretty quickly. So I suppose it wasn't really love."

"Did you guys kiss?"

She smiles sheepishly now. "Well, what do you think?"

I nod. "I think you did." Then I decide to press further. "Anything else?"

Her cheeks start to glow a little and suddenly I'm thinking

maybe I hit pay dirt. "Well, I won't deny that he wanted to do more — a lot more in fact — but I wasn't comfortable with it. So I just said no." She gets thoughtful now. "Come to think of it, that might have something to do with his finding another girlfriend."

I laugh. "Sounds like not much of a loss for you."

"No, it sure wasn't. When I think I could've ended up married to someone like Michael Stuart instead of your dad, well, it's just too scary to think about."

So there you have it, my mom's "love stories." Not terribly interesting, but perhaps there is something to be learned there. And I suppose it's something to weigh against Shawna's stories. Although I have a feeling that things were a lot different back when my mom was in high school, back in the previous century even! I have to wonder how she'd have done if she'd been a teenager in *this* millennium. Because, if you ask me, nothing seems perfectly clear, or black and white, or right or wrong.

twelve

WHY SHOULD ANYTHING SURPRISE ME ANYMORE? BUT I ADMIT TO BEING a little stunned when, once again, I discovered Shawna and Todd in the wardrobe room. Only today they were actually doing *it*. Not that doing *it* is any more shocking than that other disgusting activity, but it still makes your eyebrows lift when you walk in on a couple who are in the middle of the *act. Arggh!*

But at least this time, I managed to walk away without totally coming unglued. Honestly, I didn't even freak. I'd gone to the wardrobe room to get another skirt. You see, we have to wear these "prairie skirts" to rehearse in now. Actually, they're just long poofy things made out of calico fabric and elastic. Mrs. Hynes, the dance-team supervisor, insists we need to get the feel of dancing with long skirts (since our costumes will be like that) so she had someone sew up all these ugly things, and we wear them over tights and leotards. But, as luck or fate would have it, just as Justin was doing a lift in our dance number, my elastic sprung loose and my skirt slid right down to the floor. Of course, everyone laughed and teased, but I didn't really mind since my character is pretty much a clown anyway. I'll take any laughs I can get.

"Go get another skirt, Zoë!" yelled Mrs. Hynes, as if it was my personal fault that the cheesy thing had fallen apart in the first place.

So I dashed off to the wardrobe room and turned on the light and, *voila!* there they were again, the two rats just going at it. Well, I simply grabbed a skirt out of the box, and then for effect, I made what I hoped sounded like a disgusted sigh. Then I flipped off the light, shut the door, and dashed back to the stage.

And now I'm thinking, *like whatever, if those two need to act like that right here at school, well, who really cares?* And I'm certainly not about to tell Emily. Like she'd even believe me anyway.

Still, I must admit that I find it pretty distasteful, and my respect for Shawna is sinking. And Todd, in my opinion, is a selfish jerk. But, of course, I will keep these thoughts to myself. Or so I think. As it turns out, I can't help but spill the beans to Justin as he drives me home that night.

Naturally, he just laughs. "Man, Zoë," he finally says, "you seem to have a real knack for walking in on those two."

"Hey," I say defensively, "it's not my fault."

"But catching them both times." He chuckles.

"I have a feeling they do it all the time," I tell him. "If you ever poked around in the wardrobe room or a few other places backstage, you'd probably find them too."

He grins. "Might be interesting."

Then I sock him in the arm. "Pervert!"

"Hey, I'm just a healthy, normal guy."

I lean back into the seat, fold my arms across my chest and just roll my eyes. "*Whatever.*"

"I gotta wonder why you're so obsessed with Shawna and Todd." His tone suggests there is something wrong with me.

"I am not *obsessed*!"

"Could've fooled me."

"It's just gross walking in on them all the time. I mean what's wrong with those two? Maybe they should just get a room."

"Yeah, I have to agree with you there."

Well, I suppose that's a relief. At least Justin is showing some good sense.

"And if a teacher walked in on them." He let out a low whistle. "Man, they'd be in big trouble."

"I just don't see why they can't control themselves."

He laughs again and I start to wonder if I'm only good for comic relief.

"I'm serious, Justin. I think it's disgusting. I have totally lost respect for Todd."

"What about Shawna?"

"Well, of course, but at least she's not two-timing someone." I sigh. "What is it with guys anyway?"

"You think guys are the only ones who cheat?"

I shrug. "I don't know about this personally. But according to what I've heard, it's not that unusual."

"Girls cheat too." Now he has a look on his face that makes me wonder if someone, maybe even Katy, cheated on him.

"Has a girl ever cheated on you?"

"Maybe."

"Seriously?" I sit up straight now and study him. I mean Justin does not seem like the kind of guy any girl would cheat on.

"It happens, Zoë."

"Was it Katy?" I know I'm prying, but we're a couple now and I think I have a right to know.

He just shrugs and turns on the CD player. I suspect this is a hint that he'd rather not talk about this. Still, I persist. "Come on, Justin, you can tell me. Did Katy cheat on you?"

"I think so," he admits.

I reach over and rub the back of his neck. "I'm sorry," I tell him in my most sympathetic voice. "That must've been hard."

He nods. "Yeah, it's kind of an ego basher."

"But it's not like it's your fault," I say. "She's the one who didn't have her head on right." Then I take it to another level. "I'd never cheat on you."

He turns and looks at me as he waits for the light to change. "You wouldn't?"

"Of course not."

Then he smiles. "You're one in a million, Zoë."

And I feel my heart doing a little meltdown just then, and as if to seal the compliment he leans over and gives me a sweet kiss. We are interrupted by the honking of horns and discover the light's turned green.

"Want to go to the game tonight?" he asks as he pulls up in front of my house.

"Yeah, sure," I say as I reach for my bag.

Then he walks me to the door and gives me a longer kiss. "Pick you up a little before eight?"

"Sounds perfect."

I wave goodbye and watch Justin leave, and I'm thinking he's just about perfect as I go in my house. But to my surprise my parents have on their coats and what appear to be overnight bags sitting by the door.

"What's up?" I ask.

"Dad's taking us to Pine Tree," my mom says with a big smile.

"Us?" I question.

"Yeah," Dad glances at his watch. "Get your stuff ready and we'll pick up something to eat on the way."

"But I already have plans," I tell them.

"Plans that are better than skiing?"

"Well . . . ," I frown. "Skiing sounds great and everything, but I really wanted to go to the game tonight—"

"Oh, you can go to a game anytime," my dad assures me. "We're talking about six inches of new powder, honey."

Now I'm struggling. I mean skiing usually sounds great to me, but I'd really like to go to the game with Justin tonight. Still, I know I'm losing this argument. Then I remember something. Now if I can play my cards right. . . . "That does sound good," I tell them, acting like I really do want to go. "But what about the soup kitchen tomorrow?"

My mom frowns. "Oh, I forgot all about that. But maybe you can call and excuse yourself this one time."

"I don't know, Mom. They were really shorthanded last weekend, and I've heard the flu is still going around. I'd hate to let them down."

Dad nods. "That wouldn't be right." Then he starts taking off his coat.

"But that doesn't mean you can't go," I tell them. "I mean look at you guys, you're all ready and you probably have reservations and everything."

"Yes, but—"

"And besides, you've let me stay home alone before," I remind them.

"But that was when your sisters were here."

I laugh. "Yeah, like last year when it was just Amy and me when you went to that conference. Well, do you want to know who was babysitting who that weekend?"

Mom frowns. "That's okay, Zoë, we can guess." Then she looks at Dad. "Zoë is a level-headed girl," she says as if I'm not standing right there. "She's always been dependable and responsible."

Dad chews on this for a minute then finally agrees. "All right, I guess it would be okay. We'll check in with you regularly," he tells me, "just to make sure you're okay."

"And if anything goes wrong," says my mom, "just call the Caldwells next door. I already asked Mrs. Caldwell to pick up our paper and keep an eye on things. In fact, I better call her and let her know you'll be here."

"And if you're not at home," says Dad, "keep your cell phone on so we can reach you."

"Yeah, yeah. And don't accept candy from strangers and don't take any—"

"All right," my mom cuts me off. "We know you'll make good decisions and be perfectly fine."

Then I hug them both and tell them to have a good time.

"Oh, I better give you my car keys," says Mom, "so you can get to the soup kitchen tomorrow."

"And maybe the mall?" I ask hopefully.

"Yes, but that's all," she says. "Unless you call me to okay it."

"And we may decide to come home tomorrow night," my dad calls as they go out the door.

"Okay," I answer, but I suspect he's just saying that to keep me on my toes. Whatever. "Have fun!" I yell as I close the door behind them.

And then they are gone and I'm thinking, *this is great!* I have the whole house to myself for the entire weekend. *Woo-hoo!* Oh, it's not like I'll throw any wild parties or anything crazy, but it's pretty cool feeling like an adult, like I can be trusted to take care of myself for a couple of days. This is another one of those perks for being the youngest kid in the family!

A nervous energy pulses through me as I shower and carefully dress for tonight's date. Oh, it's not like I really think anything *big* is going to happen between Justin and me tonight, but I guess you could say that I'm open. Well, sort of open. I'm not even sure why I'm having this change of attitude. Maybe it's just this feeling of being on my own, being a grown-up, or even hormones! And, who knows, it could be related to finding Todd and Shawna in the wardrobe room today. I mean as distasteful as it was, I suppose it did get me to thinking again. And I remember how Shawna said having sex was no big deal. Apparently almost *everyone* thinks it's no big deal. And maybe they're right. Maybe it is no big deal. And maybe it's time for me to really grow up.

To everyone's surprise, our basketball team wins in the last seconds of the game, and we are all feeling pretty jazzed as we meet at Chevy's to celebrate. And I am feeling more festive than usual tonight since my friends (well, other than Emily, who really seems to be in a snit) are treating me just like old times. And then Justin selects a couple of funny old songs on the jukebox and we get up and do one of our *Oklahoma!* dances, which makes everyone just howl with laughter. It's like we're the stars of the show tonight and we're both just eating it up. I honestly can't remember when I've had so much fun.

Finally, the place is shutting down and I really wish the party could continue. But everyone is getting on their coats and heading to their cars.

"That was so great," I tell Justin as he drives toward my house. "Too bad Chevy's has to close at eleven." Now I'm about to tell Justin that my parents aren't home, and actually invite him to come in and hang for a while. Maybe see what happens between us. I guess I'm feeling a little reckless. But before I can get the words out of my mouth, he speaks.

"It's probably a good thing they threw us out," he says. "I've got my SATs in the morning and I should probably get a good night's rest."

"Oh, yeah." I chuck my romantic plans out the window. What was I thinking anyway?

"And then Dad plans to drive me over to his alma mater. He thinks if he gives me the grand tour that I'll get excited about going there."

"That should be interesting."

"I guess."

"When do you get back?" I'm hoping it'll be in time for us to do something tomorrow night, the last evening of my little bachelorette weekend. We could still have some fun.

"Dad wants to spend the night there," he informs me. "He's already arranged to stay with one of his college buddies, who's a professor there. Part of the brainwashing program, I'm sure."

"Oh." But not wanting to sound like a wet blanket, I add, "But it's a good opportunity, Justin. It should give you a real idea of what the college and campus are really like."

"Yeah, I guess. And my dad thinks I'll be able to play football there, but I'm not so sure since they're a pretty big school. But maybe I should check it out."

And so that's it. I gave up a perfectly good ski weekend for one relatively short date with Justin. Although, it was a fun one, I'll admit. And now all I have to look forward to tomorrow is the soup kitchen. Oh, man!

When we get to my house, Justin walks me to the door as usual. He stops on the porch for our ritual kiss (rather, make-out session), and I realize that we really don't have to stand out on the porch in the freezing cold. Before he can kiss me, I pull a key from my purse, quickly unlock the door, and tell him to come in.

"Huh?" he looks surprised.

"It's warmer in here," I say with a grin. "Besides, my parents aren't home."

So we go inside and stand in the entryway and kiss for a while. Then I finally say, "I know you need to call it an early night."

He nods reluctantly. "Yeah."

Then I give him a sexy little smile. "Which is too bad since my parents have left me home alone for the entire weekend."

I watch with amusement as his eyes grow wide and hopeful, then he just shakes his head and groans. "It figures!"

Now I laugh. "Hey, it's okay. I understand. SATs are important. And college is important."

"This is so unfair!"

Now I give him a little push toward the door. "Don't worry about it, Justin," I assure him. "We'll have other times. You just get a good night's sleep and do your best on that test tomorrow."

"How am I supposed to sleep knowing that you're over here all by yourself?"

I'm giggling as I continue shoving him toward the door. It's kind of fun feeling like this wasted weekend's not my fault. "Don't even think about it."

"Yeah, you bet."

I open the door and smile.

"What about next weekend?" he asks hopefully.

"What about it?" I say. Then I realize by the hungry look in his eyes that he's probably thinking of more than just a regular date and I quickly say, "I'm pretty sure my parents won't be going anywhere again."

He nods. "Yeah, I figured as much. But what about if you and I have some kind of a special date, Zoë?"

"What do you mean?" But even as I ask, I think I know.

He pulls me close again and the cold air from the open door is rushing in now. "We've been together for three weeks," he says in a low voice. "Don't you think we should do something special to celebrate?" Then he kisses me again.

"Maybe so," I answer in a slightly breathless voice.

He smiles. "Good. Just knowing that will help me to get through this weekend."

I nod. "Yeah, me too."

And so we finally say good-night and I head to bed feeling a mixture of relief and disappointment. To distract myself, I turn on my TV and watch a couple of old reruns of *Friends*. Naturally, they are both about sex. Who's getting it. Who's not. And, of course, the sympathy definitely lies with the ones who are not. Which, I suppose would be me and Justin tonight. Well, next weekend is only seven days away.

thirteen

NATURALLY, I THOUGHT AHEAD TO SET MY ALARM IN TIME TO GET UP FOR my soup kitchen duty. Now I wish I'd forgotten as I drag my weary body out of bed and step into the shower. Sleeping in until nine thirty is better than nothing, but how I miss those Saturdays when I used to sleep in until noon. Well, there's always tomorrow.

Things progress as usual at the soup kitchen, but as I help to serve, I find myself watching for that girl who's about my age. I don't know if she'll show up here again, but I'm curious about her. I wonder how it is she's ended up in a life like this. Finally, just as the last of the line passes through, I spy her standing behind a heavy-set man wearing a plaid woolen shirt over several layers of clothes. Once again, she has on the pink ski parka, only today it looks a little more grimy than last week. And her face looks even sadder. She doesn't even look up when I greet her.

"You were almost too late," I continue talking to her, even though she seems to be ignoring me. "But there's still plenty."

"Huh?" she finally looks up with empty-looking eyes.

"I was just saying that even though you're late, there's still plenty of food. And enough for seconds," I assure her as I put a heaping pile of spaghetti on her plate. "If you eat fast that is."

She sighs. "Yeah, I'll keep that in mind." But her voice is flat and hard and I can tell she doesn't really want to talk to me.

"Want an extra piece of garlic bread?" I offer.

She studies me then nods.

"It's really good," I say. "I snuck some in the kitchen earlier."

"Uh-huh."

Without being obvious, I watch her as she goes to an empty seat in the far corner. She doesn't speak to anyone. I wonder where she lives and if she has any family. I have so many questions I'd like to ask her, but I suspect it would be rude. Still, I am fascinated by her.

Soon people begin coming up for seconds and the food is going faster than I expected. I can tell that this girl isn't going to get any unless she hurries. And then we put the dessert out, which actually looks pretty good today. It's carrot cake that was donated from a local store and it has real cream-cheese frosting. I know since I sampled a little piece earlier. Okay, I forgot to have breakfast and was hungry today.

"We don't muzzle the ox that treads the corn," said Mavis when she caught me taking a small slice.

"Huh?" I looked up guiltily.

"When you work, you should eat," she told me as if it was perfectly clear.

"Oh, yeah, thanks."

Anyway, I notice that the carrot cake is quickly disappearing too. I suspect some have taken more than one piece. And so I put aside a good-sized chunk and set a paper napkin over it.

"What's this?" asks Mavis as she comes out to take in a tray of dirty dishes. I see that she's pointing at the camouflaged cake. "Don't tell me you're saving that for yourself?" She frowns.

"No," I say quietly. "It's for that girl over there. She came in late and didn't get seconds and I was worried she wouldn't get—"

"Good for you, child." She pats me on the back. "Why don't you go take it over to her? Maybe visit with her for a while and see if there's anything we can do to help her."

"To help her?" I look curiously at Mavis now. "What do you mean?"

"I mean she looks too young to be living on the streets, and maybe she'd be interested in some other options."

"What other options?"

"Oh, I don't know for sure," she says, "but the church has been known to help people out in the past. Pastor Leon believes that it's our responsibility to take care of people who can't take care of themselves."

"I'll go see if she'll talk to me," I say as I pick up the cake. "But she doesn't seem too friendly."

"Good thing that you're friendly enough to make up for that." Mavis winks at me and gives me a little push.

The girl doesn't even look up as I walk toward her. Finally I just tap her on the shoulder. "Hi," I say in a cheerful voice, "I saved this for you." Then I sit down across from her. I sense other people looking at me, but I focus my attention on her. "It's really good," I tell her as I set the plate in front of her, "real cream-cheese frosting."

"You sampled it too?" she asks.

"Yeah, couldn't help myself." I smile. "I forgot to have breakfast."

"You and me both," she says in a slightly sarcastic tone.

"My name's Zoë."

"I'm Shannon," she says as she forks into the cake.

"That's a pretty name."

"It's supposed to be Irish."

"Then it goes with your hair." She frowns as if that's an insult. "And I happen to think your hair is gorgeous."

She looks up now. "Yeah, you said that last week."

"It's so long."

She shrugs. "Can't afford to go to the salon every week anymore."

I suspect she's jerking my chain again. "I wish I could get mine to grow that long. But I always wimp out and cut it before it does."

"I've considered trying to sell my hair," she says.

"Seriously?"

"Yeah, a lady told me I could get good money for it. She also told me to keep it hidden when I'm sleeping in case someone else gets the idea of cutting it to sell."

I nod and attempt to conceal my shock that someone might cut off your hair while you sleep. "So where do you stay?" I ask.

"Here and there." She finishes the last bite and sets her fork on the plate. "The mission only lets you stay for a week at a time. And sometimes they're full up anyway. But I know my way around. I know a few places."

I lean forward now. "Do you ever get scared?" I ask.

She looks at me like I'm not too bright then says, "I'm always scared."

I frown. "That's too bad."

"Why are you asking me all this anyway?" She's scowling now, like maybe I've crossed over some line. "You doing a school paper or something?"

I shake my head. "I'm just curious. I figured you must be about my age and—"

"How old are you?"

"Almost seventeen."

"I turned seventeen a few weeks ago."

"What about school?" I ask.

"What about it?"

"Don't you go?"

"I got my GED."

I nod. "That's good. But how about college?"

That makes her laugh.

"You seem smart—"

"Yeah," she interrupts, "smart enough to get myself knocked up and kicked out of my home."

"Oh."

"So does that answer your question, Zoë?" Her tone is sharp now, as if I'd only spoken to her like she was some kind of research project.

"I just wondered if there was anything we could do to help." I offer. "I mean the church likes to help people and—"

"And you're being the good little Christian girl to come out here and give the poor sinner girl a helping hand so that you can look good on Sunday and—"

"Hey," I say quickly, "I'm not a good little Christian girl." I glance around. "Crud, I'm not even a Christian."

This seems to interest her. "What are you doing here then?"

"My parents go to this church and I volunteered to help in the soup kitchen to get out of church on Sundays."

This makes her smile. "Oh."

"But I've heard that this church likes to help people and you caught my eye and I thought maybe you'd be interested in getting some help."

"Look," she says in a firm voice. "I appreciate your offer, Zoë, but I came from a Christian home. My stepmom was such a good Christian that she couldn't stand to have a sinner like me living under the same roof. Other than a free meal on Saturday, I'm not into getting any kind of help from the church."

I nod as if I understand. And on some levels I think I do. But at the same time I feel like I really want to help this girl. But how?

"Okay," I finally say. "But since I don't really go to this church, and I'm not a Christian, how about getting some help from me?"

She seems almost interested and this gives me an idea. "Just a minute, okay?" I look at her. "Now don't leave yet." Then I hurry to the kitchen where my purse is stashed in a closet that Mavis makes sure no one gets into. I dig around until I find the Banana Republic gift card from my grandma. And thankfully, I see that she didn't write my name on it. Then I hurry back out, relieved that Shannon is still there.

"I know this isn't enough to get much," I say as I hand her the vinyl card. "But I want you to have it. Okay?"

"What is it?"

"It's just like cash, but you can only use it at Banana Republic."

Her eyebrows lift. "Banana Republic?"

I shrug. "My grandma sent it to me for Christmas, but I'd really like you to have it." I look at her pink ski jacket and, hoping that I don't sound too degrading, I say, "Maybe you could get yourself a new jacket or something warm. I think they're having their winter clearance sales now."

She brightens. "You think this jacket is pretty ugly too?" I nod sheepishly. "I got it at the mission," she admits. "I didn't have time to pack when I left home."

"Did your stepmom really throw you out?" I ask.

"Pretty much." She uses her finger to wipe the last bit of frosting from her plate.

"Are you still pregnant?"

She looks down. "No, thanks to Planned Parenthood's charity plan, I am child-free now."

"Are you okay about that?"

"Yeah, you know what they say . . . it's a woman's right to choose." Then she sighs. "What other choice did I really have?"

"I don't know." Then I reach over and put my hand on hers. "I know it probably seems kind of weird, Shannon, but I really would like to be your friend. I'd like to help you if I can."

She looks as if she's about to cry now, and I wonder if I've said something wrong. But finally, she says, "Thanks, but there's probably nothing you can do."

Now I'm feeling torn. I mean my parents are gone and I am seriously considering inviting this homeless girl home with me. I'd call them, but it's only two o'clock and I'm guessing they could be out on the slopes right now. Besides I hate to get them all worried. I study Shannon for a moment. I mean for all I know she could be a thief or a murderer. But somehow I don't think so. Mostly I think she's a girl who's hit hard times and has nowhere to turn.

"Do you want to come home with me?" I offer.

"What?"

"Just for the day, you know," I say quickly since I realize I can't exactly offer my parents' home as full-time shelter without their permission. "You could have a shower and do your laundry and stuff."

She studies me now, almost as if she's trying to figure out my motives. I mean for all she knows I could be about to sell her as a slave or something. I saw a news show where this actually happens, although it's usually in big cities. Finally, she says, "Okay, that sounds good."

So after I finish helping in the kitchen I go out and she's still there. She has a backpack and a duffle bag and I help her load these into my mom's car. Okay, I'm feeling a little nervous now, but at the same time I'm thinking this is the right thing to do.

Once we get home, she takes a shower and puts her dirty laundry in the washing machine, then falls asleep on the couch in the family room. She's sleeping so soundly that I figure she must be exhausted.

My dad calls around five and asks how I'm doing. "Okay," I tell him. "I hope you don't mind that I have a friend over."

"A *friend*?" his voice sounds slightly concerned and I suspect he thinks I'm talking about Justin.

"A girl I met at the church today," I say quickly. "Her name is Shannon."

"Oh," he sounds greatly relieved. "That's fine, Zoë."

"And if it's okay, I thought I might ask her to spend the night."

"You met her at church?" he sounds hopeful.

"Yeah, she's really sweet. You'll like her."

"I think that's okay. And I'm sure your mother will be relieved to know you're not home alone."

And so it's settled. I'll invite her to stay the night and I won't even feel guilty about it. Oh, I realize it might be risky, since I don't really know her, although I can't imagine that she'd try anything stupid like robbing us or holding me at gunpoint or anything.

And she seems pleased when I invite her to spend the night. "Are you sure your parents won't mind?" she asks.

"No, I already talked to my dad and he said that's fine. I thought I could order out pizza if that sounds good to you."

"Oh, man, that sounds awesome."

And so we spend the evening like two normal high school girls, eating pizza and watching a movie and then pigging out on popcorn, soda, and some of my dad's stashed peanut-butter cups. And Shannon really seems to be having a good time. Then suddenly our conversation takes a serious turn.

"My life used to be kind of like this," she says in a tired voice.

"Uh-huh." I reach for another handful of popcorn then lean back into the chair and wait.

"I mean just a year ago, I never would've dreamed that I'd be living out on the streets."

I nod. "Yeah, who would?"

"Although I did threaten to run away a couple of times," she says. "And I considered it. I mean my stepmom can really be a witch sometimes."

"What happened to your real mom?"

"She died when I was thirteen."

"Sorry."

"Yeah, me too. Then my dad met Sandra, at church, of course." She makes a face. "They got married a couple of years ago, when I was fifteen. And Sandra's new mission in life was to make me into the perfect daughter. Yeah, sure!"

"That must've been hard."

"Tell me about it." She reaches for another peanut-butter cup and slowly peels off the paper. "At first I thought she was okay. And I even liked going to church things with her. But then she started getting real bossy, and the harder she pushed me, the more I pulled away. My dad pretty much just checked out."

"And how did you get pregnant?"

Shannon looks at me like I have two heads then laughs. "Oh, you know, the usual way."

"Yeah, I know. But I mean was it a boyfriend or just a one-night stand or what?"

"Well, I started dating Grayson last summer. He was out of high school and seemed like he had it all together. I mean he was so cool—he had tattoos and both ears pierced and he even rode a motorcycle, which totally freaked my dad. But he was working hard and wanted to get his own place. I mean he wasn't like a total degenerate or anything."

I laugh now. "Yeah, but my dad would probably freak about a motorcycle too."

125

"And I kind of liked getting a reaction out of my dad. I mean he was like so checked out, and like Sandra was running the show. And so when Grayson wanted to start having sex, I thought, hey, why not?" She pauses and looks at me like she's waiting for my reaction.

I just shrug. "Yeah, I can understand that. I mean almost everyone I know is sleeping with someone." Then I look down at my lap.

"You mean everyone but you?"

"Yeah, but that's about to change."

So she gets me to tell her about Justin and I almost feel relieved to spill my guts to someone who doesn't go to my school and isn't related to me. I guess I really am missing Emily these days.

"Do you love him?"

I consider this. "I guess I do." Then I look at her. "Did you love Grayson?"

She firmly shakes her head. "Not even. I mean I kind of liked him then, but I totally despise him now."

"Why?"

"Well for starters, he used me. Then when I got pregnant, he dumped me and told me it was my problem, not his. And even when Sandra kicked me out, and I went to him for help, he turned his back on me."

"What a jerk."

"Yeah. I actually had these delusions that maybe he'd want to marry me and take care of me and the baby. I mean a friend of mine had gotten pregnant earlier in the year and her boyfriend married her and he was still in high school. But it wasn't like that with Grayson. I was barely out on my own before he had a new girlfriend. That's when I decided to leave town and come here." She shakes her head. "I actually thought that I might be able to get a job or something."

"But you haven't?"

"Just a couple of temporary things. The job market's tough right now, and it's even harder when you show up for an interview looking like you just climbed out of a Dumpster, which is often the case."

"Oh." Now for the first time I was stunned by how different Shannon's life was from mine.

"Well, I'm sure you're tired. And to be honest, so am I. You have no idea how nice it is to sleep someplace where you don't have to keep one hand on your bag and the other one holding a knife."

"You carry a knife?"

"Of course. You think it'd be safe for a girl to sleep out on the streets without a weapon?"

I just shake my head. I think that's about enough information for the night. "Well, I hope you'll be comfortable down here," I tell her. "I'd give you one of my sister's rooms, but they'd probably have a fit."

"Hey, like I said, no problem. And if it's okay, I might watch TV for a while. I haven't seen TV for so long."

"That's fine. And feel free to raid the fridge if you get hungry."

"Thanks," she says as I head toward the stairs. "I mean it, Zoë, thanks for everything."

And so I go to bed with Shannon's story running through my head. I can't imagine how she must've felt to have gotten pregnant and then been betrayed by her boyfriend, and then to be thrown out. Well, I know that if I got pregnant, and I have no intention of letting this happen, my parents probably wouldn't throw me out. But on the other hand, they would both be opposed to an abortion. And there was a time when I would've been totally opposed as well. Now I'm not so sure what I'd do.

I seriously hope I never have to figure that one out.

fourteen

THE NEXT MORNING I AM SURPRISED TO DISCOVER THAT SHANNON IS GONE. And at first I am alarmed, thinking she may have helped herself to anything of value and made a quick getaway. But after carefully checking through the house, even my mom's jewelry box, I am assured that everything is in its proper place. And then I discover the note she's left on the kitchen counter and feel guilty for my suspicions.

Dear Zoë,

Thank you for your kind hospitality. I decided to get out of your hair before your parents came home today. I suspect they might not be overly thrilled to find you've been harboring a homeless person. I really do appreciate your help and you've even inspired me to try harder. I'm not sure exactly what that means, but I think something's about to change for me. I may even call my Aunt Sophie (my mom's only sister) and ask her for help. But I'm not sure yet. Who knows, I may be back at the soup kitchen by next Saturday. But I really did appreciate your help.

Love, Shannon

I'm impressed with her well-written note (see, I knew she was smart!), and I'm happy that she wants to try to change things for herself, but at the same time I'm disappointed that she's left so soon.

I actually liked having her around and had been thinking I'd ask my parents to let her stay for a while.

And when the phone rings around noon, I almost expect it to be her, maybe calling me to come pick her up. But to my complete surprise it's Emily.

"Hey," she says in a flat voice.

"Hey," I say back, waiting for her to tell me why she's calling. Hopefully not to yell at me again.

"I thought it was time to bury the hatchet," she says.

"Oh."

"I mean if you're willing."

"Sure, I'm willing."

"Well, I'm sorry I was so hard on you," she says. "I was hoping we could get together and talk. Are you busy today?"

And so we agree to go to the mall together. I'm a little nervous about her driving since last time I had to take the bus home, so I offer to take us. We get to the mall without any huge fireworks and walk through our favorite shops together, almost as if nothing was wrong. But when we sit down to have a late lunch, she begins to lay her cards on the table.

"I'm thinking you might be right about Todd," she says as she sticks her straw into her soda.

I just nod.

"I mean I think there is something going on between him and Shawna Frye."

I nod again, almost afraid to join this one-sided conversation.

"I saw the two of them together a few days ago. I got off cheerleading practice early and came down to the auditorium since Todd was going to give me a ride home that night, but I caught them out in the hallway and I'm pretty sure they were kissing."

Feeling like one of those bobble-head dolls, I just nod again. Sure, I want to say things like, "See, I told you so," and, "Todd is a total jerk," but I know enough to keep my big mouth shut.

"We got into a big fight and Todd tried to tell me they were just practicing one of their scenes. But I'm not buying it." Then she leans over and peers at me. "They wouldn't be out in the hallway practicing a kissing scene, would they?"

I suppress laughter. "No," I say, trying to sober up. "In fact, Mr. Roberts has told us to save the kissing for the actual performances."

"Yeah, I figured." Now she just sits there with the saddest expression on her face. "Well, go ahead," she tells me, "go ahead and say I told you so."

I just shrug. "That's okay. It looks like you figured it out on your own. Maybe I should've just kept my mouth shut from the start and then—"

"No way," she says. "You did the right thing. I mean you are, or at least you were, my best friend, and I should've known you wouldn't lie to me. I just didn't want to believe it. I guess I was in denial."

"Yeah, like the Queen of De Nile," I say jokingly.

"Yeah." But she still looks sad. "So, it was true then? They were really doing what you said?"

"I wouldn't make something that disgusting up."

"I know." She seems to consider the whole thing. "I mean I realize that guys don't take that stuff too seriously. I mean I've heard that they just use the girls who are willing to do that, and how guys would never get seriously involved with someone that trampy. I mean look at Monica Lewinsky. It didn't exactly get her where she wanted to be."

I shake my head. "Not hardly."

"And I suppose I could excuse Todd if he promises not to do anything like that again."

Now I feel like screaming and I'm wondering if I should just come out and tell her the rest of the story.

"I mean Hilary forgave Bill, didn't she? I suppose I could—"

"Look, Emily," I say suddenly. "You may hate me for saying this, but I can't keep pretending."

"What?"

"Well, I personally think that what Todd and Shawna did the first time was bad enough, but I actually walked in on them a second time."

Her blue eyes grow wide now. "They did it again?"

"Not exactly," I tell her. "This time they were actually having sex, you know, the old-fashioned way."

She closes her eyes and lets out a small groan.

"I'm sorry," I tell her quickly. "And you probably hate me. But I can't lie to you. I wouldn't have said anything if you hadn't called today. But, believe me, Emily, Todd *is* cheating on you."

"You actually saw them, Zoë?" Her tone is challenging again, like she thinks I could imagine this kind of thing.

"Look, Emily. I wish I hadn't seen it. Now I'm really ticked at Shawna too. And I thought she was my friend. Now I think she's almost as much of a jerk as Todd."

"Almost?"

"Well, at least Shawna isn't going with anyone else. What Todd did with her was a big slap in your face."

Now Emily starts crying and I feel terrible for being so blunt. "I'm sorry," I tell her.

She uses a paper napkin to blot her eyes. "It's not your fault, Zoë."

"I know, but the whole thing just sucks."

She continues to cry without talking and I'm feeling really uncomfortable. Finally I tell her that he's not worth it, that he's a jerk, and she should just break up with him. I actually think that she's listening and might even agree. Then she speaks.

"But don't you see?" She looks at me like I should get it, but I really don't. "Todd is my first. And I really do love him, Zoë. I honestly thought he and I would be together always. I mean my parents met while they were still in high school and they got married and it's worked for them."

"I think that's pretty rare," I tell her.

"Maybe, but I really thought it could happen."

"Todd doesn't deserve you, Emily."

Then she looks up at me with watery eyes and says, "Do you think I could've held on to him if I'd been willing to, well, you know, do more of that stuff with him? I mean like Shawna does? Do you think I was too boring?"

"Oh, Emily!" I sigh in complete exasperation. "How can you even think that? And if it's true, well, doesn't it just prove what a total jerk-faced idiot he is?"

"I don't know."

And so it went with us. We sat in the food court of the mall just going back and forth about things like monogamy and fidelity and what's okay and what's not. And, let me tell you, by the time we finished we were just as confused as when we started. No, let me change that, we were *more* confused.

It's like nothing really makes any sense when it comes to sex. It's like all the lines get blurry and fuzzy and a girl can't figure out what's right or wrong or anything in between. And the truth is that most of the messages I'm getting are saying that it's *no big deal*, that

I should just go for it and be like those good-looking and popular girls who star in *Friends*. Not that I'm saying they're tramps in their real lives, but if you add up how many guys they've all slept with on TV you'd probably hit triple digits.

But here's what's really troubling me most of all: I'm thinking that when it comes to sex, it's the girls who get hurt. Oh, I don't mean physically, although from what I hear, they don't make out too well there either. But I mean emotionally, socially, even financially (look at Shannon). In every sexual relationship I can think of (even in Thea's and Kirsti's, even though they act like it's no big deal when their boyfriends do something sleazy) it's the girls who come out hurting. And I've got to ask myself, what's up with that? And how is that fair?

So to say that I'm feeling more confused than ever is no exaggeration. And now I'm pretty worried about my promise to Justin about doing something "special" with him next weekend. And now I'm thinking that I should consider this whole thing more carefully, before it's too late to just say "no."

Not that I'm planning to say "no." But if I do go along as planned, if I do agree to have sex with him, then I want to know that I'm doing it for all the right reasons. And right now, I'm just not too sure. But I will say this, I'm really thankful this weekend went the way it did. I'm *so* glad that Justin had SATs and his college visit while my parents were away. I mean who knows what might've happened otherwise?

fifteen

As I enter the auditorium for rehearsals, Nate walks up to me and says, "I've really been praying for you, Zoë."

"Huh?" I look at him like he's got a big green booger hanging from his nose.

"Well, it was weird, I just got this really strong feeling that I should pray for you this weekend. And so I did."

"You actually *prayed* for me?" Now I feel kind of worried, like, what's this supposed to mean? Does Nate think I'm some kind of a freaky chick who needs to be prayed for? I mean if he's going to pray for someone, he should pray for someone like Shawna or Todd. Now those two are seriously messed up and probably in need of prayer. But, of course, I don't say this.

"Yeah. Maybe I shouldn't even tell you about it, but I just wondered if everything's going okay with you?"

"Sure." I feel uneasy. "Everything's just fine."

He smiles. "Good."

Good? I think it's kind of disturbing, not to mention weird. I mean Nate's a nice guy, but I don't really like the idea of him praying for me. Then I remember Shannon and I wonder if it might have had something to do with her. So I tell him about my strange overnight guest and how she took off the next day. And he seems really interested.

"That is so cool, Zoë," he says with what seems like genuine admiration. "I can't believe you'd do something like that."

"Why not?" Suddenly I feel kind of sad about the whole thing. "But I was sort of disappointed when she left like that. It seemed so sudden."

"But it sounds like she was going to do something to get off the streets," he says. "You might've saved her life."

I shrug now. "Oh, I doubt that."

"Really, Zoë, maybe that's why I was praying for you. Maybe God was using you to help her."

"Maybe." But I'm really thinking, *yeah, sure, how could God use me?* I mean I don't even give God the time of day. Still, it does make me wonder.

"Well, I'll be sure to pray for Shannon now."

I nod. "Yeah, that'd be good."

Rehearsal goes worse than usual today, like no one can get it together, and I can tell Mr. Roberts is getting seriously aggravated. Finally, he decides to call it a night and sends us all home. But not before he gives us a little lecture about how we need to take this thing seriously and how we have only four more weeks to get our acts together.

* * *

"How was the campus visit?" I ask Justin as he drives me home.

"Okay, I guess."

"Do you think you want to go there?"

"Maybe, but I don't really know why my dad's so set on it. Well, other than the fact that he went there. The only good thing I can see is that I'd only be a couple hours from home."

"That's great," I say in a cheerful voice. "Maybe I could even come up and visit you sometime."

He nods.

"And how about your SATs?" I ask. "You never said how that went."

He kind of frowns. "Who knows?"

"Well, did you feel okay about it?"

"Not really."

"Don't worry. I always feel the worst about the tests I end up acing."

"But you're a better student than I am."

I feel surprised by this. "How do you know that?"

He shrugs. "I can tell."

Now I'm feeling bad for him. He really seems down. "You shouldn't think about it too much, Justin," I tell him. "It won't do any good to worry."

He nods. "Yeah, you're right." Then he brightens. "Are we still on for Saturday night?"

I really want to tell him that I'm still thinking this whole thing over, but then I hate to disappoint him, especially when he's already feeling so bummed right now. "Sure," I say. "Looking forward to it."

Then he reaches over and places his hand on my knee, giving it a little squeeze. "Me too."

And so the week progresses with Justin and me. Hard play rehearsals, quick make-out sessions behind the scenes, small talk as we ride home together. Then the same old same old the next day. Am I getting bored with him? I'm not sure. Maybe I'm just looking for an excuse to bail on Saturday night. I don't know.

* * *

On Thursday, Casey stumbles upon Justin and me making out behind one of the straw bales that we're using for part of the set.

"I am getting so sick of this," she says as we pull ourselves apart.

"Huh?" I mutter without looking her in the eyes.

"Everyone sneaking around and kissing and stuff. You'd think they put something in the school's water."

Justin laughs as he pulls a piece of straw from my hair. "Yeah, someone dumped love potion into the Hamilton High water system. Don't you ever drink water, Casey?"

She just rolls her eyes and walks off. And, even though I know Casey is kind of a nerd, I still feel guilty about getting caught like this. It reminds me of the times I walked in on Shawna and Todd. Thankfully that hasn't happened lately. In fact, I haven't even seen them hanging together. I wonder if Emily's little talk with Todd did some good after all.

Still, I think if I had to confront a boyfriend about something like that, well, what would be the use? Why not just lose the loser? I wonder what I'd do if Justin did that to me? He's a pretty cool boyfriend, but I don't think I'd stick around and take it like that. At least I hope I wouldn't. I'm not sure why Emily doesn't just give Todd his walking papers.

Justin has to leave early today for some family thing, and I am left on my own for the remainder of practice, which also means I need to figure out a way to get home. I'd consider asking Shawna, but I've been really avoiding her this week. Actually, she might be avoiding me too.

I find a quiet corner during one of my breaks and think I might actually catch a quick nap when I am joined by Casey. I brace myself as she starts to chatter at me. As expected, it's her usual lecture about how she is saving herself for that special guy and her wedding night.

And I suppose I deserve this abuse after getting caught by her behind the hay bale, but finally I decide that enough is enough!

"Look," I say to her, hoping I can cut this off. "I'm really sorry you found Justin and me kissing back there, but it really doesn't have anything to do with you, okay?"

"Oh, I know that, Zoë," she says, like she's Miss Congeniality. "But like I've said, you seem like a nice girl, and I don't get why you'd want to mess around with someone like Justin."

"Ex*cuse* me?" I try to use a fairly insulting tone now. I mean this girl does *not* seem to get it. I thought I'd made myself clear about her dissing Justin like this.

"Oh, I'm not trying to judge Justin, but you know he has a repu-tation, and I don't see why you — "

"Who doesn't have a reputation?" I suddenly wish I hadn't asked. Even an idiot can see where she'll take this.

She points to herself. "Moi."

"You *do* have a reputation, Casey. It just doesn't have anything to do with sex."

"The thing is, Zoë," she continues, totally oblivious that I'd rather be talking to a stone than to her, "God has a plan for our lives. He has someone really special picked out for you, and if you waste yourself on someone else, you'll be sorry when the real thing comes along."

"When the real thing comes along?" I frown at her. "That sounds like a TV ad."

"I mean when God brings your future husband into your life." She points her finger at me now, a practice I can barely tolerate in anyone. "How are you going to feel when the man you truly love, the man you want to spend the rest of your life with, have children with, comes along and you have to tell him that you've already had sex with who knows how many other men?"

Well, how do you respond to something like that? I mean all I can do is just sit there and stare at her as I wonder, *What planet did this chick beam down from? And when is she going back?*

"I'm serious, Zoë." This girl is relentless. "What are you going to tell him?"

"Who?" I ask dumbly.

"Your future husband."

I shake my head. "I don't know my future husband."

"But when you meet him, when you're engaged, about to be married . . . what are you going to tell him about the guys you've slept with and—"

"Hey," I say defensively. "I haven't slept with—" Then I stop myself. Why should I tell Casey that I'm still a virgin, especially when most of my friends think I'm not?

"See," she says triumphantly. "It makes you uncomfortable, doesn't it?"

"*You* make me uncomfortable," I tell her as I stand up.

"It's not me, Zoë," she says with confidence. "It's God."

Well, I don't even respond to that as I walk over to the drinking fountain and take a long cool drink. I can't believe that Casey Renwick, of all people, is able to push my buttons like that. What is up with her?

"Casey getting to you?" asks Nate from behind me.

I stand up, wipe my mouth, and stare at him. "Don't tell me you're going to pick up where she left off," I say in a fairly hostile voice. "What? Do you Christians have some kind of game plan to drive the rest of us bonkers until we fall down our knees and beg God to help us?"

He laughs. "Not really. But it might be worth a shot."

"Yeah, you bet."

"Hey, I'm sorry if Casey comes on too strong. But she probably thinks she's doing it for God's sake."

"Well, for God's sake, I wish she'd knock it off."

"Me too."

"She acts like she knows what's best for everyone."

Nate seems to consider this then nods. "A lot of Christians make that same mistake."

"Do you?"

"Oh, yeah, lots of times. But I'm trying to break the habit."

"How's that?"

"Well, I'm trying to think about the way that Jesus dealt with stuff," he tells me as we sit in the back row of the auditorium.

"What do you mean?" I ask.

"Like he'd come across someone who was obviously blowing it and he wouldn't get mad at the person or call them names or act like he was superior."

"What would he do?"

"Become their friend."

A little light goes on. "Oh," I say. "Is that why you're trying to be my friend?"

He looks slightly sheepish. "Well, I wish I could say that it was because of God, Zoë. But the truth is, I've always thought you were pretty cool. I always wanted to get to know you."

Somehow this makes me feel better. "Thanks," I tell him. "So, you're not really trying to convert me or anything?"

"That's God's business," he says. "I just want to be your friend."

"Well, that's cool." I glance at my watch now and realize it's close to quitting time. "Hey, friend, do you want to give me a ride home?"

"Sure, no problem."

And so I find myself riding home in Nate's old clunker pickup. He tells me that he likes it because it has a canopy in back where he and his band can stow their stuff when they're doing a gig somewhere.

"People actually pay you to play?" I ask.

He frowns then laughs. "Yeah, I suppose it seems unlikely."

"No, that's not what I meant," I quickly tell him. "I just didn't know if there'd be much money in religious music."

"We don't call it religious music," he says.

"Christian music?" I try.

"It's just music that's played by guys who love God," he says in a slightly weary voice, like maybe he's had to explain this before.

Now I feel sort of bad. "I actually thought you guys were really good at the soup kitchen," I say. "And if I hadn't known it was you I probably wouldn't even have known you guys were Christians."

Now he really laughs. "You seem to have some pretty judgmental thoughts when it comes to Christians, Zoë. Why is that?"

I consider this. "I'm not sure. I mean my parents are Christians and I think they're pretty cool. And you're a Christian and I think you're cool."

He smiles now. "Thanks."

"But then there are people like Casey Renwick." I make a face. "She just makes me want to run screaming from God."

"But she's just one person."

"Then there was my fifth-grade Sunday school teacher," I begin to say and wish I hadn't. I thought I'd forgotten about that woman.

"And?"

"Well, she was this uptight lady who got mad about everything, and she even made this boy cry one day because he forgot to bring his offering."

"That's too bad."

"And she was so mean that I quit wanting to go to church, and

I decided that God wasn't very nice if he let people like Mrs. Daniels teach Sunday school." Now I feel kind of silly, like this is no reason to turn my back on God. So I continue. "And then I got older and I read about things that have happened during history, things that were done in the name of Christianity. Things like the Crusades where innocent people were murdered for not being Catholic. Or wars over religion. I mean even Hitler claimed that God was on his side. I finally just got totally sick of the whole religion thing."

"Do you believe that God controls people? That he made them do those evil things like Crusades and religious wars?"

I consider this and feel fairly certain that God isn't controlling me like that, so how could he control anyone else? "Probably not."

"So is it fair to blame God for other peoples' bad choices and mistakes?"

"Maybe not."

"And do you think God was pleased with all that crud? Like the Crusades and killing and wars?"

I just shake my head no. "Turn on this street," I tell him in a quiet voice.

"Sorry," he says as he turns. "I guess I'm as bad as Casey. I really didn't mean to preach at you, Zoë."

We're at my house now and I feel slightly offended by the lecture, but I'm not exactly mad at him. "It's okay, Nate," I say as I reach for the door handle. "If anything I suppose you've made me think."

"Thinking's okay," he says with a smile. "Right?"

I smile back at him. "Yeah, thinking's probably okay."

"Mostly I just wanted to tell you that I think God has a really great plan for your life, Zoë. I mean you're such a cool girl, and the way you helped Shannon, and volunteer at the soup kitchen . . . well, I just think that God has big plans for you."

Well, I'm not too sure what that means, but at least it sounds encouraging. "Thanks for the ride," I tell him as I climb from the pickup.

And so, between Casey Renwick and Nate Stein, I suppose I am thinking about God a bit more today. And I'm wondering if God really does have a plan for my life. Well, it's kind of mind-boggling, but I guess I'm curious. It's not like my own plans are anything to brag about these days.

sixteen

NEW GOSSIP BREAKS OUT ON FRIDAY MORNING AND IT'S NOT LONG BEFORE everyone is talking about it.

I get the scoop during second period. "Did you hear about Shawna?" Kirsti asks me during English lit. We're supposed to be reading *Ivanhoe*, but Mr. Franklin has stepped out for a minute. That's when I glance around the room and notice that Shawna is absent.

"What happened?" Maybe Shawna's been in a car wreck or something tragic, which makes me feel horrible, since I've been so snooty to her all week.

I can tell Kirsti is thrilled that I haven't heard yet. She loves to be the one to spill bad news. "Well, remember how Andrea's cousin Caleb goes to Jackson High?"

"Yeah."

"It seems he told Andrea that Shawna transferred from their school because she has some horrible STD and she was too embarrassed to keep going there."

"STD?" That sounds familiar, but I'm kind of stuck as I ask myself what those initials stand for.

"Sexually transmitted disease."

"Oh, yeah." Now I feel stupid.

"I guess it's a really bad kind that takes special medication to treat but never totally goes away." Then in true Kirsti fashion she goes into all this gory and graphic detail.

"Eww!" I make a face at her and hold up my hands to make her stop. "Too much information!"

"Well, that's what happens, Zoë." She looks at me like I'm a baby, but I don't even care.

"Yeah, whatever." But now I remember what Shawna and Todd have been doing during play rehearsal and I'm feeling worried. "But you say it's *really* contagious?" I ask Kirsti and she gives me this "would I lie to you?" nod. So I glance over to where Emily is sitting just a few seats from me and I notice that she seems unusually focused on her book, especially considering that Mr. Franklin is nowhere to be seen. But as I watch more carefully I can tell that her eyes aren't moving over the words. She's not even reading! That's how I know she's heard the news about Shawna too. Poor Emily.

I try to comfort her at lunch, but she doesn't want to talk about it. And when the other girls seem unable to shut up, Emily just splits.

"I don't see what *her* problem is," says Thea in an aggravated tone. "I mean we have a right to talk about this and be worried for our own sakes. I've heard that Shawna's a real tramp and I happen to know that Brett has been cheating on me with someone. For all I know it could be little Miss STD."

"Oh, Thea," says Andrea with exasperation. "You make me wish I'd never told anyone." She slowly shakes her head and sighs loudly. "The only reason I did was so that you guys could watch out. I mean the way *some people* act, it could turn into an epidemic around here."

"Duh," says Kirsti, who turns her attention back to Thea now. "So have you asked Brett if he's been with her?"

"Yeah, but he denies it."

"Guys always deny it," says Kirsti, who's also looking a little uneasy.

And so it goes until I can't take this discussion anymore. I slip away and go off in search of Justin. I haven't seen him since this morning when he gave me a ride to school, and we barely talked then. But now I wonder if he's heard the news and if so, what's his reaction? I remember how he thought I was making too big a deal over Todd and Shawna. But what does he have to say about that now? Finally I find him by his locker, but it's almost time for fifth period.

"Hey, babe," he says, smiling as he reaches to give me a hug.

"What's up?" I ask. "Where were you during lunch?"

"I went to a college recruiting meeting in the counseling center," he tells me. "This college sounds like a pretty cool place and because they're kind of small I might even be able to apply for a football scholarship."

"That's cool." Then I ask if he's heard about Shawna yet.

He rolls his eyes. "Who hasn't?"

"Don't you think that's awful?" I say.

He just shrugs. "It happens."

"But she might've infected Todd," I say quietly enough that no one can hear me. "And, who knows, he could've infected Emily—"

"And Emily could've infected Josh and—"

I punch him in the arm now. "Hey, watch what you say about my best friend."

"Well, you're the one who got going on this whole thing."

Just then the bell rings and our conversation comes to an end. Still, I feel a little disturbed by his response. Like he honestly thinks it's no big deal.

Due to an overly zealous soccer match in PE, I don't actually get to talk to Emily until we're in the locker room. "How are you doing?"

I ask quietly, before the other girls start piling in around us.

I can tell by her red eyes that she's been crying. "I'm getting by," she says.

"Have you talked to Todd yet?"

She shakes her head. "What am I supposed to say?"

"Hey," says Thea as she throws her damp towel at Emily. "What are you so bummed about, girlfriend?"

Emily forces a pitiful smile. "Can't you cut a girl some slack for being premenstrual?"

"*Premenstrual*," teases Kirsti. "You sound just like my mom only she's *premenopausal*. It's like everyone's got an excuse."

"Give her a break," I say.

So then they set their sights on me and start quizzing me about Justin. Like have we done *it* yet, and how that boy won't wait forever on me, and if I'm not interested in his body, well, there are plenty of other girls who are. I'm totally sick of their big mouths.

"I'd think you guys would lighten up," I say too loudly.

"What for?" demands Thea, standing there in nothing but her scanty bra and panties. "What's your problem anyway, Zoë?"

"I just think that in light of this thing with Shawna, well, you guys might want to rethink some of your favorite activities. If you know what I mean."

Their silence tells me I've rocked their world just a bit. Plus Andrea gives me a subtle thumbs-up like she's backing me on this. So there.

Unfortunately this little reprieve doesn't last long.

"Oh, I just think Zoë's premenstrual too," says Kirsti.

"Yeah," agrees Thea. "You girls should take some Midol and Tums and call me in the morning."

So I throw my soggy wadded-up towel at Thea and smack her

right in the head, which results in a completely immature towel-snapping, wedgie-giving, locker-room episode straight out of middle school. Finally, we are all laughing so hard that we can barely stand up. And I know there are no hard feelings. But when I look around, I notice that Emily's gone.

Moods seem subdued at play practice and Mr. Roberts is seriously aggravated that Shawna is gone.

"Do you know where she is, Zoë?" he asks. As if I'm her personal bodyguard or something.

I make a blank face and tell him that she's been absent all day. Then several people snicker like that's really funny. I glance over to where Todd is leaning against a partially constructed wagon that's part of our set. I'm relieved to see that he's not laughing. In fact, he looks rather serious, especially for Todd.

"Do you think this is going to ruin the play?" I quietly ask Justin, but he just shrugs.

Soon we are rehearsing and I am thankful to be distracted from the realities of life by the silliness of this corny musical. But then it's time for me to take a break. Justin is working on his rope tricks to use in the dance number. And I find a seat on a straw bale where I can sit and watch. Once again I am impressed by his talent. If he doesn't make it into college he could probably head out to Texas and get a job on a ranch. Yee-haw!

"I heard about Shawna." Nate sits down next to me on the bale.

I glance at him. "Yeah, I think everyone's heard it by now."

"Everyone but Mr. Roberts."

"That's just a matter of time." I feel thoroughly discouraged now. Not just about Emily, but I'm also worried about this musical. We've put so much work into it, and now the star has vanished. "Do you think it'll hurt the play?" I ask.

"Nah," he says. "I'm guessing the talk will die down and Shawna will be back and everything will turn back to normal. At least on the surface."

"But underneath?"

He sighs now. "Well, that's a heavy load for her to be carrying."

"I can't believe she had sex with Todd knowing that she was contagious." I don't even try to hide my disgust.

"Someone must've done the same thing to her."

"I can't believe you can excuse her like that! Especially considering that you're Christian. I mean you can't honestly think that what she did was okay." I glance over to Casey Renwick now and wonder if she knows what's up with Shawna. "I'm sure Casey would be happy to give Shawna a piece of her mind."

"I'm not saying that I think what Shawna did was okay, Zoë. I'm just saying that everyone makes mistakes. Jesus was in a situation like this once. These guys brought a woman to him who'd been caught sleeping with someone who wasn't her husband."

This sounds vaguely familiar, but I'm not really sure how it goes. So I bite. "And what did Jesus do?"

"Well, the law of the land was to stone the woman. And Jesus told them to go ahead, but to let the guy who'd never sinned begin the stoning."

"Oh, yeah," I say. "I remember that."

"The point is, we've all blown it, Zoë."

"Yeah, I know. But it's like Shawna's recklessness could take everyone down with her."

"That's the way it goes sometimes."

"I can't believe how complacent you sound, Nate."

"It's not complacency, Zoë."

"What is it then?"

"I don't know. I guess I don't see the point in getting all bent out of shape over someone blowing it. I mean I'm praying for Shawna and I hope she gets her act together. But I sure don't hate her for what she did."

I consider this. And I suppose if I were to admit the truth, I'd have to say I hate her. Right now, I really, really hate her. Oh, I hate Todd too. But I think I hate Shawna more. I wish she'd never transferred to our school. More than that, I wish I'd never befriended her. And, in some ways, I suppose I feel like I'm partially to blame for this mess. Still, I'm not going to admit this to Nate or anyone.

* * *

"Want to go to the game tonight?" Justin asks as he drives me home after practice.

"Sure," I tell him. Then I ask him more about the college he's suddenly interested in and discover that it's about six hundred miles from our town. "Wow," I say. "That probably means you won't be coming home much next year."

He nods. "Yeah, it's a long drive and I'm sure the airfare could start to add up. But I probably won't even get accepted there anyway."

"But you might," I tell him. "And it'd be cool if you got a football scholarship."

He brightens. "Yeah, that'd be awesome."

I act like I think it'd be great, but I'm really wondering if he has the slightest concern about being so far away from me. Maybe we're not as close as I assumed.

"I'll pick you up before eight," he says as he pulls up at my house. "I'd walk you to the door, but I better hurry if I'm going to get a shower and get back here in time."

"No problem," I say as I hop out of his car. Even so, I'm starting to wonder if I'm not seeing the writing on the wall. Just the same, I take a shower, get dressed, and grab a quick bite to eat.

"You guys staying in tonight?" I ask as I see my parents comfortably settled in the family room. They're both on the couch and Mom has her feet in Dad's lap and he's rubbing them and they both look perfectly content.

Mom nods. "Just a couple of old fogies, I guess."

"Nice old fogies," I say. And I'd never admit this to anyone, but I sort of admire what they have. Okay, it might be kind of boring, but it's sweet.

Our basketball team doesn't do as well as last week, but it's still a good game and, as usual, we go to Chevy's afterward. I notice right away that Emily and Todd are missing. And it's like their absence leaves a real hole in our group of friends. As a result it's not long before girls like Kirsti and Thea start talking.

"What's up with those two?" Thea asks me in the bathroom.

I just shrug and say I don't know.

"I think that Todd's been cheating on her," says Kirsti.

"Give it a rest," says Andrea as she checks her mascara in the mirror.

"No, I'm serious," says Kirsti in a listen-to-me tone. She glances around the small bathroom as if to see if anyone else can hear, then says in a quiet voice, "I heard from a somewhat reliable source that Todd may have been involved with Shawna Frye."

Naturally this stuns everyone. Well, everyone but me, and I'm not talking.

"No way," says Andrea.

"Way," says Kirsti.

"Do you think Todd slept with Shawna?" says Thea with wide

eyes. "And then slept with Emily?"

"I agree with Andrea," I say as I move to the door. "You guys should just give it a rest."

"But what about—"

I don't hear the rest of the sentence because I'm out the door with Andrea following.

"Good move," says Andrea as we join the guys at the table.

I give her a little smile, but almost wish that I could tell her the truth. I have a feeling she'd understand. Still, my loyalty lies with Emily and I know this isn't my story to tell.

"Can you and Justin teach Jamie and me that dance you guys did last week?" asks Andrea.

And so we manage to break the somewhat somber mood by picking some funny old big band songs from the jukebox, and then Justin and I teach everyone how to do the swing step. And for a while it's like we've all really gone back in time. And I wonder if maybe life really was simpler back then. I almost wish we could all get warped back into a more innocent era. Or maybe there's no such thing.

But when the evening finally ends, I am feeling like Justin and I are as solid as ever. In fact, there's this sweet little episode when Brett wants to switch partners and dance with me, but Justin gets all protective and refuses. And suddenly I'm thinking I don't need to be worried about this guy. I can tell he really cares about me.

"We're still on for tomorrow night?" he says after we've stood kissing on my front porch for longer than usual. "For our anniversary celebration?"

I nod and attempt to catch my breath.

"I made reservations for Chez Lavelle's," he tells me as he gently runs his hand over my hair. "You might want to dress up."

"Sounds great," I say and then we kiss again.

Finally he steps back, but then he takes both my hands in his. "I really do love you, Zoë," he says in a voice that cracks just slightly.

"Oh, Justin!" I say as I throw my arms around him again. But for some reason I don't tell him that I love him too. It's like I can't quite bring those words to the surface yet.

We kiss a bit more and then say good-night. And I go into the house to find that my parents have already gone to bed. And I walk up the stairs feeling like I'm slightly starry-eyed and dizzy, almost like I'm intoxicated but without wanting to hurl. And suddenly I wonder, could *this* be love?

seventeen

To my surprise, Nate is also working in the soup kitchen on Saturday. We visit and joke as we do mundane chores like peeling apples and scrubbing carrots, but I'm relieved that our conversation never gets too serious. It's not that I don't appreciate the things we've talked about in the past. And it's cool how Nate can get me to think. But today I just don't really want to think.

"I hear someone's phone ringing in the closet," calls Mavis from where she's chopping onions.

Thinking it must be mine since no one else is checking, I go and dig through my bag and finally answer.

"I was about to give up on you," says Andrea.

"What's up?" I ask as I pick an apple peel off my jeans.

"It's an emergency," she says, although her voice sounds calm.

"Emergency?" I say loudly enough to get Mavis' attention.

"We need to get Emily out of her house today," Andrea says. "She's totally bummed and needs to be cheered up."

"Yeah?"

"Can you meet us at the mall at two?"

And so I agree to meet them in the food court. Andrea is calling it "Mission Emily," but I wonder if she knows the half of it. I'm not even sure that I do.

"Something wrong?" asks Nate when I rejoin him at our apple-peeling station at the sink.

"Andrea and I are going to try to cheer up Emily today."

He nods as he tosses another peeled apple into the bowl. "That's cool."

"Yeah. Andrea's calling it Mission Emily, but I'm worried that it might be Mission Impossible."

We finally finish serving, and I work as fast as I can to help get the kitchen all scrubbed and ready for next week. Shannon didn't show up today. I'm hopeful this means she's taken some steps in a promising direction.

"It was good having you with us today, Nate," says Mavis as we all start to leave. "You just let me know if you want this to be a regular thing."

He laughs. "I don't know if I can commit to that since our band usually practices on Saturdays, but I don't mind being on call when you're shorthanded." Then he reaches in his jacket pocket. "Which reminds me, we got these business cards made for the band, you know, but they have my cell phone number on it. Just in case you can't reach me at home." He hands one to Mavis.

"Well, look at that," she says, pausing in the parking lot to study the card. "And so professional looking too."

"Let me see," I say.

"Here," offers Nate. "You can have one too. We've got like a thousand of them."

"Thanks," I say as I glance at the card then slip it into my sweat-shirt pocket.

"Just in case you ever need to call me." He winks.

"Right." I kind of laugh. Like I'd ever need to call Nate about anything.

Then I try not to speed over to the mall. I put on some cologne at the stoplight since I'm pretty sure I still smell like onions. Then I slap on some fresh lip gloss as I hurry inside. Andrea and Emily are already seated at a table on the second level. They're both sipping coffee and look slightly uneasy.

"Sorry I'm late," I say as I sit down.

"We got you a mocha," says Andrea as she slides the cup in my direction. "It might still be hot."

"Thanks." I take a sip to find that it's only lukewarm. But I don't complain. "How's it going, Em?"

She just sighs and looks down.

"Can't get her to talk," says Andrea, looking concerned.

"Did you tell Emily about the rumor that started circulating last night?" I ask.

Andrea's eyes grow big as she shakes her head no. "I, uh, was waiting for you to get here."

"Well, don't worry. Emily already knows."

Emily looks more interested. "Knows what?"

"Kirsti got it into her head that Todd may have cheated on you with Shawna," begins Andrea.

Emily rolls her eyes now. "I figured it was just a matter of time."

"So, it's true?" asks Andrea.

Emily shrugs.

"Did you talk to Todd yet?" I ask.

"I haven't seen him around."

"But don't you think that's kind of suspicious?"

"I don't know." Now Emily is looking irritated. "Maybe you're the one who's suspicious, Zoë."

I frown.

"It was Kirsti who started the rumor," says Andrea.

Emily gives her a skeptical look. "Don't be so sure."

"Look, Emily," I say. "If you're saying that I started the rumor, you better take it back. You're the only one I ever told." Then I remember something. "Well, other than Justin."

Emily points her finger at me. "So maybe Justin leaked it."

"Oh, I don't think—"

"But you don't know, do you, Zoë?" Emily looks at me with eyes that are full of angry tears. "You don't know anything."

"But I saw them," I say. "And not just once."

Her fists are tightly clenched now. "So you say."

"Oh, Emily." I glance over at Andrea who looks somewhat shocked by this revelation. "I wouldn't make something like that up. Besides, I'm not the only one who saw them."

Emily looks alarmed now. "Who else saw them?"

"Casey Renwick."

She frowns.

"And she's not exactly the kind of girl who'd make something like *that* up."

"Whatever." Emily looks slightly stumped as she fidgets with her empty cup.

"Why don't you just call him?" I suggest. "Just ask him and get everything out in the open?"

"Look," she says to me. "I know that Todd's not perfect. And maybe he was flirting with Shawna, or whatever. But nobody's perfect, Zoë." Now she narrows her eyes. "Everyone sure knows that your boyfriend isn't."

"What do you mean by that?" Now I'm feeling seriously irked. Who's she to go pointing the finger at Justin?

"Come on, you guys," says Andrea. "This is getting too—"

"What do I mean?" says Emily. "Don't you remember what

happened last summer when he was two-timing Amber with Katy?"

I kind of blink.

"Yeah," she says as if she's just won a huge victory. "Memories can be convenient, can't they? Well, don't forget that Justin isn't any better than Todd. And you're still with him, aren't you?"

"But that's different. I wasn't going with Justin way back then. He's never cheated on me. But you know that Todd's cheated on you." I grab her hand now and make her look at me. "And he's cheated with someone who has a very contagious STD, Emily! That's a whole lot different. I just hope he hasn't given it to you!"

Now her eyes are flaming and I know I've gone too far.

Way too far. I also know, or at least I suspect, that it is too late. I mean Emily and I are pretty close, and I can tell by her expression that, despite my warnings, she has probably had sex with Todd since the Shawna factor moved in. I feel equal portions of anger, sadness, and concern.

"Thank you very much for that helpful information," she says in an icy voice as she stands up and reaches for her bag. Then she turns and walks off. Just like that.

"Oh, man," I say as I put my head in my hands. "I guess I really blew that."

"Is it true?" asks Andrea, sounding stunned. "Did you actually catch Todd and Shawna together?"

Well, it's not like this is some big secret anymore. Besides, of all people, Andrea is probably the most trustworthy. So I tell her the whole sordid story.

"I can't believe it."

"I know," I agree. "And neither could Emily. But it's true. I mean why would I make up something like that?"

"No way. I mean you and Emily have been best friends for like forever. Still, it's too bad. I feel sorry for Emily."

"And I told her the very first time I caught them."

"But she wouldn't listen."

"It just makes me so mad. It's like she trusted Todd more than me. Like I would lie to her. And then she has the nerve to compare Todd and Justin. Like Justin would do something like—like that." And suddenly I find that I'm crying too. I sort of expect that Andrea will say something reassuring, that she'll comfort me and remind me that Justin's not like that. But she just sits there watching me.

Finally I stop crying and use a paper napkin to blow my nose. "Sorry," I tell her. "It's just so upsetting."

She nods. "I know."

"And I think it was sleazy of Emily to drag Justin and me into her mess. I mean it's our three-week anniversary this weekend," I say. "And we're going out to celebrate tonight. And all this crud about Todd and Shawna . . . well, it's like a great big wet blanket. You know?"

Now Andrea looks concerned.

"What's wrong?" I ask.

"Oh, nothing." She glances around uncomfortably.

"No, it's something. What?"

"Well, Justin's a nice guy, Zoë. And I know you guys haven't been together that long, but . . ."

"But what?"

"Oh, I should probably just shut up."

"Not now. You know something. Spit it out."

So, in her tactful Andrea way, she tells me that Katy was indeed pregnant and that she really did have an abortion.

I'm not sure how to respond. "How do you know?"

"Katy told me."

"Oh." I consider this. "But you don't know that Justin was the father—"

"He was."

"But he told me that Katy had been cheating on him. Maybe the guy she'd cheated with—"

"Katy never cheated on Justin."

Something about the way she says that seems to imply something more. "Are you saying that Justin cheated on Katy?"

She gets an expression that could best be translated as "duh."

"Well, I know there was that rumor about Thea," I begin. I feel like I'm drowning now, and grabbing for something—anything to keep me afloat. "But that was ages ago and . . ."

"Katy told me that Thea wasn't the only one, Zoë."

"Why are you telling me this?" I feel fresh tears coming and, like Emily, I am ready to walk out.

"For the same reasons you told Emily what you saw. You're my friend, Zoë. You're a good person and I think you deserve to know what's up."

"Are you saying that you think Justin is cheating on me?" I finally manage to ask.

"No," she assures me. "Not at all. As far as I can see, Justin seems totally smitten by you."

I feel a small wave of relief. "And isn't it possible that he's done some regrettable things in the past, but that he could change?"

She nods. "Of course. And hopefully that's what's happened. Maybe I was wrong, Zoë. But I just felt you should know. Was that wrong?"

"I don't know," I say. "Maybe not."

"Really, Zoë, I didn't mean to bum you. But if it were me, I'd really want to know. I mean if Jamie was doing something that might hurt me . . . You know what I mean?"

I consider this. "I guess. But, lucky for you, Jamie seems to be about the only guy who hasn't messed up."

She shrugs this off, as if she's not so convinced. "Well, you never really know, do you?"

Well, I for one, do not feel like cruising the mall now. In fact, I feel so exhausted that all I want to do is go home and sleep this all away.

"Sorry that Mission Emily blew up on us," she says as we clear our table and start to leave.

"It was a nice try," I tell her.

"And, really, don't let what I said get you down. Okay?"

"Yeah, sure."

"Just be smart," she says with a smile. "And have a good time with Justin tonight."

"Thanks."

But I don't know if that's even possible now. In fact, I feel like I don't know much of anything at the moment. But my plan is to take a long nap and just forget about everything for a couple of hours. And maybe I'll wake up with a perfectly clear head and all of life's answers to all of life's questions will be laid out right in front of me. Yeah, sure!

eighteen

I WAKE UP FROM MY NAP FEELING SURPRISINGLY HAPPY AND WHEN I TRY to figure out why, I remember that I'd just been enjoying the most delicious dream about Justin. We were at Disneyland together and we'd just gotten off a water ride, which had gotten us so soaked that we had to change clothes. And then I came out wearing this Cinderella costume and Justin was Prince Charming. And we had this great embrace with music and everything.

Okay, it was sort of hokey. But it was also very romantic and sweet. And suddenly I feel like our date tonight will be perfectly wonderful.

Thanks to my sister Amy, I have my outfit all planned for tonight. I went perusing her closet last week, just in case she left anything interesting behind. As it turned out, she did. Naturally, she didn't forget to take any of her good everyday clothes, but she did leave a few of her dressier things behind. And this one dress, a retro number right out of the fifties, seemed to be calling my name. Naturally, I phoned to ask her permission to borrow it and she was perfectly fine with it. "But watch out," she warned me in a teasing voice. "That's one hot little dress." Of course, I just laughed. But now that I have it on, I think I know what she means. Like wow! I hadn't considered that I'm a little more "well endowed" (as Mom puts it) than Amy. But this slightly low-cut bodice really accentuates this fact. The dress is red satin with spaghetti straps and a tight waist with a full skirt that swooshes when you walk.

Now some people (like Mom) might expect me to wear a fancy pair of shoes with a dress like this, but this is where my sense of humor (or lack of fashion sense) kicks in, because I've decided to wear my red-and-black cowboy boots. I guess I don't want to look *too* sexy tonight. Especially when I'm not totally sure where the evening is going. Or isn't going. Besides, I do have my own personality. To further make this point, I top this outfit with my black zippered, hooded sweatshirt—although I do put a retro pin on it, which I think adds a touch of class. Then I put my hair into a high pony tail that I backcomb for fun. And although the whole thing may sound a little weird, I happen to think that I'm stylin'.

"Interesting outfit," says my dad when I come downstairs. I can tell by his expression that he's not sure what to think.

But I just grin. "Thanks, I like it." And then Justin is here and I'm telling my parents good-night.

"Hey," says Justin as he gives me a kiss just outside the door. "You look like fun."

I laugh and give my ponytail a toss. "I feel like fun."

Then I notice he seems to be holding something behind his back. "I know this is kind of corny, but I wanted to get you something for our anniversary."

"What?" I say eagerly.

He pulls out a corsage. "It's to wear on your wrist," he says, and I can tell he feels silly.

"It's beautiful." I hold out my wrist so he can slip it on. "Thanks."

Then he opens the door to a car I've never seen before. It's a dark-colored Mercedes that smells brand new.

"Whose car?" I ask after he gets into the driver's side.

"My folks let me borrow it." He smiles. "Thought it might be nicer than my old Blazer."

"Very uptown," I say as I run my hand down the smooth leather upholstery.

"Yeah, we're living high tonight."

And so it seems we are. He pulls right up to the entrance of the restaurant (which is on the lower level of a very fancy hotel) and a valet takes his car keys and then Justin comes over and opens my door, takes me by the hand, and we walk through a spacious lobby where there is an enormous fountain, and marble floors, and large vases of real flowers, and velvety couches and chairs, and suddenly I'm feeling like a real, live princess.

We enter the restaurant now, and that's when I notice that Justin has a small black backpack with him. I think this is kind of odd, but he winks at me as he checks it to the coat clerk, along with my sweatshirt. I fumble not to destroy my wrist corsage during this little transition.

Then it's not long, because he had reservations, before we are seated at a candlelit table. I notice a few heads turn to take in my dress as we walk by. We're not far from the dance floor, and a grand piano played by a middle-aged man wearing a tuxedo with tails. Little white lights go around the perimeter of the wooden floor, but no one is dancing yet.

All in all, this place is very, very elegant. And suddenly I'm wondering if the cowboy boots were a bad move, but I quickly forget about this once we start to order. Justin seems to have it all figured out, and since I'm already over my head (I mean my parents never eat at places this ritzy—at least not when I'm with them) I just sit back and let him order for me too. Fortunately I know enough to follow his lead when it comes to using the right silverware. By the time our entrée is served, I think I'm doing okay.

"Have you eaten here before?" I ask, trying not to reveal how impressed I am by all this grandeur.

He nods. "Yeah, my dad likes the food here."

"I can understand that. It's really delicious."

"We usually just come for birthdays or special occasions."

"Well, this feels like a pretty special occasion to me," I say as I study him in the candlelight. Justin looks surprisingly sophisticated in a dark jacket and striped tie. I think it's the first time I've ever seen him this dressed up. Oh, maybe at a dance before, but he would've been with Katy then, and I probably would've been watching from a distance and wishing that he was with me. Well, tonight he is. He really is!

"You look so pretty, Zoë," he tells me.

I'm glad I checked my sweatshirt with the coat lady now.

As we're waiting for our desserts to arrive, I notice that several couples are beginning to dance.

"Want to try out their dance floor?" asks Justin.

"Sure."

And so we join the other couples, all old enough to be our parents, but we hold our own with them (due to all our *Oklahoma!* rehearsals). And when it's all said and done, the older couples smile at us and I can tell they're impressed that we actually know our way around the dance floor.

"That was fun," I tell Justin as we return to our table in time to see our waiter lighting our dessert on fire.

I suppress a shriek of delight (I mean I am trying to appear somewhat sophisticated) as I watch the flames fly high. The waiter seems pleased by my shocked reaction and offers me the first piece of something that had the word flambé in it, although I don't recall the whole name. But I'm not disappointed because it really is delicious.

We dance again and then return to our table for coffee.

"I wish this evening could go on forever," I say in a dreamy voice.

"No need for it to end yet," he says.

Then he pays the bill (even leaving a generous tip) and we dance a couple more times before we go get my sweatshirt and his backpack. Then we go back out to the spacious hotel lobby. We walk around for a bit, just holding hands and admiring the fountain and a small art exhibit along one wall. Then I notice the women's restroom and excuse myself.

I think it's the most beautiful restroom I've ever seen. Everything is marble and gold (at least it looks like gold) and there are bottles of lotion, perfume, and all sorts of things lined up on the big counter. And instead of paper towels or obnoxious dryers, they have real cloth hand towels rolled up neatly in a big basket. I had to watch to see another woman dry her hands and then she just threw the barely used towel into a hamper beneath the counter. Fascinating. Okay, I'm sure I'm spending way too much time in here.

I go back into the hotel lobby but don't see Justin. And so I just wander around, figuring he must've found something equally interesting in the men's room. Finally, I hear him calling my name and I spot him on the other side of the fountain.

I go over to join him. "This place is awesome. You should've seen the women's bathroom." Then I laugh. "Well, maybe not."

"Come on," he tells me. "I have a surprise." Then he leads me to the elevator where we ride up to the seventeenth floor.

"Where are we going?" I ask, feeling a little nervous.

"You'll see."

We walk down a wide hallway that's lined with pieces of ornate antique furniture that are either topped with beautiful lamps or flower arrangements. Then Justin stops in front of room 1733 and slips in a key card and opens the door.

"Presto!" he says as he swings the door open. He flips on a light switch to reveal a room that's every bit as elegant as the rest of this place.

"But why?" I ask as I slowly walk into the room, realization sinking in as the big bed comes into view.

He grins as he closes the door then pulls me toward him. "So we can be alone." He leans in to kiss me.

I kiss him back, but I'm thinking, *Hey, wait a minute.* "You should've told me you were planning this," I say, trying to keep my voice even.

"Hey, just relax, Zoë," he says as he sets his backpack on the table by the window. Then he pulls open the drapes to reveal the city lights stretched out below us.

I look out, feeling a mixture of excitement and terror. "That's pretty," I say in a voice that doesn't even sound like me. Then a loud bang makes me just about jump out of my cowboy boots. "What's that?" I shriek as I turn around to see who shot the gun. But all I see is Justin holding what must be a bottle of champagne, and it's overflowing onto the rug. I run to the bathroom and grab a towel and attempt to sop it up.

"Don't worry about that," he says as he fills two glasses. "They'll take care of it later."

I set the towel on the table and just stand there feeling perplexed. What should I say? How should I act? I know what he's expecting from me. I'm just not sure I can (or want) to deliver.

"Here." He hands me a full glass of champagne and holding his glass up says, "To our first three weeks."

Feeling like a puppet, I hold up my glass, hear it clink against his, then, following his lead, I take a sip. I've never tasted champagne before and for some reason I thought it would be better than this. But I don't let on that I think it tastes like fizzy vinegar. Instead I brace myself and take another sip. Then I say, "Justin, I didn't know that you wanted—"

"Don't talk yet," he says in a hushed voice. He pulls out a chair for me, next to the window. Then he goes over and turns on some music, fiddling with the stations until he finds one that plays lighter tunes. Now he comes back and sits opposite me. Leaning back and putting his feet on the low table between us, he says. "Let's just enjoy the view." He takes another sip. "And the evening."

So we sit there and I listen to all the chatter in my head. It's like there's this big argument going on in there. One side is saying that Justin is my boyfriend, he's treated me to a special date, and this is my big chance to lose my status as one of the few remaining virgins at Hamilton High. The other side is reminding me of all the crud that I've witnessed lately, and how Justin may have been responsible for Katy's pregnancy and subsequent abortion. And back and forth I go, barely hearing Justin's next question.

"Zoë?" he says again.

"What?" I look at him blankly.

He's holding the bottle of champagne out. "Ready for more?" he asks hopefully.

Well, I've only had a couple of sips, but I nod and hold out my glass anyway. And he fills it nearly to the top again.

I take another cautious sip and this time it doesn't taste quite as bad as before. Still, I think it must be an acquired taste. Finally, I know I have to say something.

"You've kind of caught me by surprise," I say, taking another sip of my champagne to make him feel better.

"What do you mean?" he says as he fills his glass again. "We talked about this last week."

"We talked about doing something special," I remind him. Of course, at the time, I had a pretty good idea of what that "something special" might be. But tonight I guess I just want to play dumb.

"Yeah," he says. "And that's what this was supposed to be." He gets a disappointed look on his face now. "Don't you think this has been pretty special?"

Okay, now I feel really guilty. "Of course," I assure him, "it's been totally awesome. Dinner was amazing. Dancing was incredible. But I'm just not sure about"—I glance around until my eyes stop at the king-sized bed—"this."

"So you were just leading me on?"

Now I feel torn. Was I really leading him on? Did I know that this evening was destined to end up in a hotel room? I'm not even sure. I stand up and begin to pace across the room, trying to keep my eyes off that bed. "I don't know, Justin," I finally say. "I guess I should've known this was part of the deal."

He sets his glass down now and, standing up, he faces me. "I thought we had something special, Zoë."

"We do."

"Then what's the problem?"

"I'm not sure."

Then he reaches for me and pulls me toward him. "Just relax," he tells me. And then we begin to slow dance. And I'm not sure if it's the champagne or feeling his body close to mine, but I do begin to relax.

Then as we're dancing I feel his hands searching over my dress and I realize that he's looking for the zipper, which I am relieved to remember is tucked discretely on the side. But then I feel his hands moving over the folds of my full skirt, trying to lift it up. And that's when I step back.

"Don't," I tell him.

He looks shocked. "Don't what?"

"Don't start trying to undress me," I say in what I know must sound like a very uptight voice. I sit down in the chair again, folding my arms across my chest. "I'm not ready for that."

He flops down in the chair across from me and exhales loudly. *"So when are you going to be ready, Zoë?"* But there's something about the way he says those words, and something about the hard look in his eyes that makes me feel even more uncomfortable.

"Look, Justin. I've had a good time with you this evening, but there are some things that are bothering me."

"Like what?"

"Well . . ." Of course, I'm not sure how to best say this and finally I just blurt it out. "Andrea told me that Katy really was pregnant, and that she had an abortion, and that it was your baby. She also says that you're the one who cheated on her."

Justin stands up now. His fists are clenched and for a moment I think he is going to hit me. "And you believe her?"

I step back. "Why would she lie to me?"

"How would I know?" Then he cusses. "But you're taking her word over mine?"

"I don't know. . . ."

"Then why are you telling me this?"

"Because it's bugging me. And if we're in a serious relationship, I have a right to know the truth. Think about what's going on at school right now. Someone like Shawna goes around sharing her STD and—"

"I've never *been* with Shawna!"

"I'm not saying you have, Justin." Now I'm feeling really angry. Like what right does he have to put me in this position anyway? "I'm just saying that *if* I'm going to have sex with you, and that's a *big* if right now, then I have a right to know who you've been involved with and what happened."

"Says you." Now he goes over to his backpack and pulls out another bottle. Only this one isn't champagne. It looks like something a lot stronger. And he pours himself a tumbler full of the brownish liquid and takes a big swig.

I watch him slug down that drink and pour himself another and suddenly I'm feeling extremely nervous. I know I don't want to stay here with him, but if he keeps drinking like a fish, I don't want him driving me home either.

"I'm sorry, Justin," I say in what I think sounds like a calm tone. "But I think I better leave." I begin to walk toward the door, but before I get there he grabs me by the arm.

"Where do you think you're going?"

"Home." I study him evenly.

"Not yet you aren't." Then he pulls me toward him and begins kissing me. Besides the fact that his kiss is wet and sloppy, his breath smells like something my dad might use to clean his tires. I push him away and tell him to let me go. But his grip only tightens and now I am seriously scared. I mean I've heard of date rape before — even Shawna warned me about it. If anyone has ever put herself into a bad position, it is me, and it is tonight. I consider screaming for help, but really that seems so juvenile, and what if no one could hear me and I only made him angrier? Besides, I'm not stupid, and I'm not drunk. I should be able to get myself out of this.

He is pulling me toward the bed now. "I paid lots of money for this date and I'm not finished yet." And it becomes painfully clear, as he pushes me onto the bed, this guy's not only in great shape, but he probably outweighs me by at least eighty pounds. I can feel my heart racing and I know I better think fast, before it's too late. I consider kicking him with my cowboy boots, but am afraid if it turns to violence, I'll be on the losing end.

"Hey, slow it down," I tell him, trying to sound calm as I think through a quickly contrived plan. I run my fingers through his hair now, just for effect. Then I reach up and pulling his face toward me, I kiss him again. Long and hard, like I really mean it. Then I gently push him away. "Let's do this thing right, Justin," I whisper, hoping to sound sexy and interested.

"Okay, babe," he says eagerly. "I thought you'd see it my way."

"I do," I tell him. "It just takes me a while to get into it, you know. You just need to slow things down a little, okay?"

"Sure, babe, we can take it slow if you want." But his hand is already pushing my skirt up now, attempting to feel beneath my dress.

"Hang on, Justin," I tell him as I move his hand from my leg. "I mean if we're going to do this, let's make it enjoyable. I want to remember this night for a long time."

He backs off a little now. "Okay," he says, pushing some hair out of his face. "What do you want?"

"Well, first of all, I'd like to get into something more comfortable. This dress is kind of tight."

He smiles. "Yeah, I noticed."

"I thought I saw some terry robes by the bathroom," I tell him. "Do you mind if I change into one of them?"

He smiles now. "Not at all, babe. Make yourself at home. *Mi casa es su casa.*"

"Okay," I say with my best smile. "Why don't you pour me

another glass of champagne while I change?"

"You got it, babe."

So I walk toward the bathroom, which is near the door. Then, grabbing my sweatshirt, I head straight for the door and quietly let myself out. I'm not sure if he heard, but I waste no time heading for the elevator. And to my relief there's another couple already waiting there. At least Justin won't be able to make a scene if he catches up with me.

My heart is still pounding as I ride the elevator down. I try not to look at the couple as they hold hands and look at each other like star-crossed lovers. I mean if love is anything like what I just experienced in room 1733, well, they can have it! Finally, I am in the lobby. But what should I do now? Who should I call? If I'd thought to bring a purse (which I felt certain would spoil my outfit) I could hire a taxi. Expensive maybe, but worth it. As it is, I don't even have my cell phone with me tonight. How stupid could I be?

I know I could, maybe should, call my parents, but I really don't want to. For one thing, this is so totally humiliating. I mean what are they going to think, having to pick me up at a hotel? And what do I tell them? How do I explain what happened to Justin? I put on my sweatshirt and stuff my hand into the pockets as I walk over to one of the phones, which I assume are for guests to use. But then I'm a guest, aren't I? Like Justin said, he paid plenty for that room. I try not to think of what he might be doing now. Perhaps riding the elevator down, ready to grab me by my ponytail and drag me kicking and screaming back to his room.

My hand nervously fingers something in my pocket and I pull it out to discover it's the business card that Nate gave me at the soup kitchen today. I look at the phone number on it and wonder if he was serious about that "call anytime" bit. Well, it's worth a try. So I dial his number thinking he'll probably be doing a gig with his band, or maybe he's out on a date with (I'm sure) some nice Christian girl, maybe Casey Renwick. No, besides the fact that she doesn't date, she's not even his type. But I'm so shocked when he answers on the second ring that I start crying, and then I blubber out this totally lame explanation for where I am and why I need his help, saying, I'm sure, way too much. What is wrong with me?

"Take a deep breath," he tells me. "And try to calm down."

"I'm sorry," I tell him. "I shouldn't have bothered you, I'll figure out some—"

"No, it's okay, Zoë," he assures me. "I'm coming to get you, but I just don't want you to fall apart before I get there."

"I—I won't," I tell him, glancing over my shoulder to make sure that Justin isn't nearby.

"I'm leaving right now," he tells me. "And I'll be there as soon as I can, but it'll still probably take about fifteen minutes. Are you in a safe place?"

"I'm in the lobby." I look around the area. "And there are people all around the place. I'll wait by the fountain. It's right in the middle."

After I hang up, I cautiously walk across the lobby and sit on a padded bench right next to the fountain. It's in direct view of the registration desk, where there seems to be a constant flow of people. To my relief, Justin doesn't make an entrance. I wonder if he even knows that I'm gone yet. Or maybe he's already drunk himself into a stupor. I feel something scratching on my wrist and remember the corsage that's now stuffed into my sleeve. I wrestle the stupid thing out and toss it into a nearby trash can. It's not like I'll be saving any mementos from this evening.

A wild mix of feelings rush through me as I wait for Nate to get there. Like why didn't I realize that something like this would happen tonight? And is it my fault? I did lead Justin on. And was it a mistake to wear such a sexy dress? Like what kind of a message did I want to send anyway?

But on the other hand, what right did Justin have to *expect* that we'd have sex? I mean just because he put out for a fancy meal and a hotel room, which he never even asked me about, does that mean I have to surrender my virginity to him? I don't think so.

And suddenly I am thinking maybe my virginity is actually worth something. Like maybe I really don't want to throw it away too easily. And I even wonder why I've been so worried about being one of the last remaining virgins on the planet. Maybe it's a good thing.

nineteen

NATE WALKS INTO THE HOTEL LOBBY AND I TRY TO REMEMBER WHEN I'VE been so glad to see anyone. Maybe back when I was five and got lost at the mall and then my mom showed up and rescued me. But that's sort of how I feel as Nate walks toward me now. Even so, I find myself looking over my shoulder, still worried that Justin might show up and make my exit difficult.

"Thanks so much for coming," I quickly tell him. "We should probably get out of here, pronto."

"Have you seen him?"

"No. I was actually hoping that he knocked himself out with whatever it was he was drinking. He had a whole bottle of champagne, plus a big bottle of something else that looked even stronger. Maybe whiskey."

"Do you think he'll be okay?"

I consider this and wonder if I even care. "I don't know. . . ."

"Maybe we should let the desk clerk know and have someone check on him."

"Oh, I'm not sure—"

"I'll call on my cell," he says as he picks up a hotel brochure from a rack just outside the door. "The phone number is right here."

And so, once we're safely inside of Nate's pickup, he asks me the room number then calls the hotel. "We're concerned about a guest in room 1733," he says in a very mature voice. "He's by himself and consuming an unhealthy amount of alcohol. Plus he's underage."

I feel my eyes growing wide at this tip. Is Nate trying to get Justin busted?

"That should take care of it," he says after he hangs up.

"But won't he get in trouble now?"

Nate starts his pickup. "Nah, the hotel wouldn't want to call the police or anything; it would make them look bad. But the underage part will probably make them feel responsible enough to check on him."

I sigh in relief and lean back into the seat. "How did you get so smart?" I ask.

"It's part of living," he tells me.

I kind of laugh. "Are you trying to tell me that you've been around stuff like this before?"

"What makes you think I haven't?"

"Let me think," I say for effect. "Maybe the fact that you're such a nice guy, not to mention a Christian?"

"That doesn't mean that I haven't been around and seen a few things."

I study him for a moment. "Are you saying that you lead some kind of double life?"

Now he laughs. "Not exactly." He's pulling out of the parking structure to the street now. "Hey, do you want to stop for a coffee or anything?"

"Sure," I say. "That would probably help to clear my head before I go home."

So he takes us to Jitters Java, a coffee shop that's a few blocks away from the hotel and I continue to question him about his double life.

"Like I said, it's not a double life," he tells me as we sit down with our coffees. "It's just that I've seen my older brother mess up a lot. I'm usually the one who has to go out and rescue him. I guess I've learned a thing or two from his mistakes."

I nod. "I have a sister like that. I've covered for her a few times, but I've never really rescued her. She usually just called my parents when she got into big trouble. I just couldn't stand to do that tonight."

He takes a sip of coffee. "Well, our mom is single and she's not a really strong person, if you know what I mean. She has her own demons to deal with."

I consider this. For some reason I just assumed that Nate came from the kind of family that you'd see sitting in the front row of church every Sunday. "Oh."

"It's not like she wouldn't do more if she could. But it's all she can do just to get herself to work every day without falling apart, you know."

I nod like I know, but I really don't. I mean my parents are like the most solid, steady people I know. I couldn't imagine what it would feel like if they weren't. Suddenly I'm realizing there's a lot more to Nate than meets the eye. "What happened to your dad?" I ask.

"The usual. He met someone he liked better than my mom. Someone who didn't have all the baggage my mom had. He lives about a thousand miles away. But at least he's fairly regular with his alimony and child support. That's something."

"I'm sorry."

He peers at me. "Why?"

"I mean about your dad, your parents . . ."

He waves his hand. "Oh, that's okay. I learned a long time ago that God makes a better father anyway."

"Huh?"

"I was thirteen when my dad ran out on us. At first I was really angry. I mean here's my mom with two boys to raise, and she's already unstable, and she didn't even have a job at the time. What kind of a jerk would do that?"

I nod and listen.

"I spent about a year being mad. You might even remember what an attitude I had during middle school."

I shrug. "I just figured you were going through something."

"Oh, I was. I really was. But that's when I met Pastor Leon. He's pretty amazing. Anyway, he got through to me and I finally gave my life to God."

"And that changed everything?" I can hear the skepticism in my voice, but Nate doesn't seem to mind.

"No, that didn't change everything." He takes another sip. "But it started changing me."

"How did it change you?" I'm actually interested in hearing this. I mean after tonight, I think there are probably some things I wouldn't mind changing about myself.

"Well, first of all, it gave me someone to talk to, someone to take my problems to—"

"You mean Pastor Leon?"

"Not exactly, although I knew he would listen. But I'm talking about a relationship with God, Zoë. It's like he really did become my father. And I could talk to him about anything. Not only that, but it's like he gave me some real direction for my life. Like I wasn't lost anymore. I had some guidelines and some idea of where I was going."

"Kind of like a compass?"

"Yeah, I guess you could say that."

I listen as Nate talks about God like he's his best friend. And, despite myself, I am being more and more drawn in.

"Lots of things changed," he continues. "Like instead of just looking at myself and feeling sorry for poor old me, I began to care about others. And the more I cared about others, the less cruddy my life seemed."

We've both finished our coffee now, but I feel like I could keep listening to him all night. How weird is that? But even weirder is this feeling that's growing inside of me. I'm not even sure how to describe it. Maybe it's hope.

"Sorry to go on and on," says Nate as he looks at his watch. "Oh, man, it's almost midnight. Do you have a curfew?"

I shrug. "My parents are pretty laid back. But I suppose I shouldn't push my luck."

"Yeah." He stands. "I should get you home."

We continue to talk as he drives me home. Suddenly I am full of questions about what he believes and how he can be so sure it's real and how did he know that he wasn't just imagining things and so on.

"It's about faith," he finally says when we're in front of my house. "It's hard to explain, but it's something God actually plants inside of you. I guess you know it when it happens."

"How do you know?" I demand, unwilling to get out of his pickup without this information. "What does it feel like?"

"It probably feels different with everyone. For me it was just this sudden burst of realization, I guess. Kind of like a hunch that you know you have to act on before you lose out. Does that make any sense?"

I nod. "A little."

"The thing is," he continues, "if God is really planting faith in you, I think you'll know it, Zoë."

"I hope so." Then I reach for the door handle. "Thanks for rescuing me tonight, Nate."

He grins. "Once again, it's Nate to the rescue."

"And thanks for everything else too." Then I get out of his warm pickup and run up to the house. I turn to look back and he's still waiting there. I guess he wants to make sure I get into my house safely. I wave at him then go inside.

My parents have already gone to bed, but my dad calls out good-night as I tiptoe to my bedroom. I answer him and go into my room and shut the door. But as I get ready for bed, I feel wide awake. Maybe it's the coffee or just the adrenaline that's still rushing through me from the events of the evening. But I know I won't be able to go to sleep for a while. I'm thinking about what Nate said. And I'm thinking about this tiny feeling of hope that keeps flickering. In light of what happened with Justin, it doesn't quite make sense. Like shouldn't I be all bummed and worried right now? But there it is, this tiny spark of something that came from who knows where Could it be from God? Could it be what Nate was calling faith?

And suddenly I am actually down on my knees. Now how weird is that? But it's like I'm caught up in this moment, like I'm afraid to let it slip by unnoticed, like I might miss out on something that could change my entire life. But I have no idea what to do now. Or what to say.

"Okay, God," I am whispering, "if what I am feeling inside of me is really you, can you please make it a little more clear? I mean can you show me that it's truly you? Or faith? Or whatever?" Then I just wait, still on my knees. I sort of expect that this feeling will vanish before long, because, to be honest, I feel sort of silly just kneeling like this. It's so out of character. Okay, maybe it was a real feeling, but it'll probably slowly diminish like a candle that's burning out. But to my amazement it not only stays with me, it seems to grow.

"Is this for real?" I whisper again. "Is this really you, God?" And to my total amazement, I have this sense that it is for real. That it is God. But, even so, I'm not sure what to do with it. Or about it. So I just stay there on my knees until I finally feel so tired that I know I'm about to fall asleep. But still it's like I'm afraid to get up and go to bed, like maybe I'll miss something or it will go away. And so I ask God to keep whatever this is going until the morning. It's not like this is a test exactly, but then maybe it is. I'm not sure. All I know is that something inside me feels vastly different. I feel a sense of hope, and I don't want it to go away.

twenty

INSTEAD OF SLEEPING IN UNTIL NOON THE NEXT MORNING, I FIND THAT I'm awake and ready to get up. And it's only nine o'clock. I shower and dress and go downstairs, where my parents are having coffee and reading the newspaper.

"You're up early," says Dad as he glances from the sports page.

"And dressed too," adds Mom. "What's the occasion?"

"I don't know," I tell them.

"Maybe you want to go to church," says my dad, but I can tell by the way he's saying it that he doesn't really think that I do.

"Yeah," I say. "Maybe I do."

Now my mom studies me like she thinks maybe I'm sick or have some huge sin to atone for or something. "Everything okay with you, Zoë?"

I force an uncomfortable smile. "Yeah, sure. Everything's fine."

And so I go to church with my parents. It's not Easter or Christmas and I am actually going to church with them. I can tell they're afraid to say anything, like maybe they'll jinx this thing and I'll change my mind at the last minute and not go inside. But I do.

We sit down and I prepare myself to listen. I mean really listen. It's like I suddenly care. Like I really want to know what Pastor Leon has to say today. And for the first time ever, it's like I really hear him. I mean I totally get him. He's talking about friendship. And how Jesus is such a devoted friend that he gave his life for his friends. He's saying that we're not just Jesus' servants, but his dear friends, and that he chose us and has a plan for us. And I am sitting on the edge of the pew thinking, yes, yes, this is how I feel inside. This all makes sense.

Then Pastor Leon does something that I've never seen him do before. (Of course, I only come to church a few times a year, so how would I know?) But he is inviting people to leave their seats and come down to the altar if they want to commit or recommit their lives to Jesus. And my heart is pounding even harder than it was last night when I was trying to escape from Justin. And I know, somehow I know, that I need to pry my rear end off this pew and walk down there. I'm just not sure that I can.

Then I consider the alternative. What if I don't get up and go down there? And suddenly I am on my feet and walking forward. And it's like everything around me is just a blur. All I can think is, *Get down to that altar and make it fast.*

I admit that I'm relieved not to be the only one. In fact it looks like nearly half of the people in church are up front. And then Pastor Leon leads us all in this prayer where we give our lives to Jesus and invite him to rule our hearts. I repeat every single word and when I'm done, I know that I meant it. I realize that tears are running down my cheeks as I walk back to my seat. But I don't even care. And then I see my parents and realize that they are crying too. We hug and I feel a little self-conscious, but really good too.

After church, Nate comes up to me and gives me a big hug. "That is so cool, Zoë," he says. "Welcome to the family."

I smile and tell him all about what happened before I went to bed last night and he totally gets it.

"I'm not sure what this means," I admit. "Like what I'm supposed to do next."

"Don't worry," he assures me. "God will lead you."

I nod. "Good. I'm ready for some direction."

* * *

Now, even though I believe that God is in my heart and I can talk to him and he is leading me, I still feel a little uneasy as I go to school on Monday. And I'm really not looking forward to speaking to Justin.

I manage to make it through half the day without actually seeing him, and when I do he just totally ignores me. And, hey, that's fine with me. I mean I knew our relationship was over the minute I ran out on him. But it's not until after PE (in the locker room of course) that I find out what he's been telling everyone.

"Hey, Zoë, sounds like you and Justin had one hot night last weekend," says Thea with a spark in her eye. Naturally, everyone else gets real quiet.

"What do you mean?" I ask as I struggle to pull a sock over my still-damp foot.

"I mean it sounds like you really delivered the goods," she says.

"Yeah," agrees Kirsti. "Too bad it wasn't *good* enough to keep him, huh?"

"Huh?" I look up at Kirsti.

She gives me this I-feel-so-sorry-for-you look. "Oh, don't feel bad. Lots of girls get dumped after delivering the goods."

Now Thea pats me on the head. "Yeah, it's okay, Zoë. You really should've left Justin to some of us more experienced women." Then she laughs.

I attempt to straighten them out, but now they're getting so carried away with themselves and their X-rated jokes that I might as well be talking to my locker. Finally I just give in and let them rip on me. Emily and Andrea look on with slightly sympathetic eyes, but they don't say anything in my defense. I suppose they think I deserve it. Even Shawna, who is back in school today and keeping totally to herself, is watching this little exchange from her safe spot on the other side of the locker room. I hurry to finish dressing then make a quick exit.

I know my cheeks are flushed with embarrassment, but more than that, I'm angry. Really, really angry! How dare Justin go around slandering me, giving me a reputation that's totally undeserved! I duck into the restroom that's near the auditorium and go into a stall and close the door. I stand there for several minutes just trying to calm myself and keep myself from crying. All I need is to go to play rehearsal looking all red-eyed and soggy. I take a deep breath and attempt to pray, but this is all still very new to me. I'm not even sure what to say or what to ask for. Finally, I just thank God for being my friend and ask him to help me through this thing. I stay in the stall a few more minutes and finally I am beginning to feel stronger and I think maybe I can survive seeing Justin at rehearsal.

When I come out of the stall I'm surprised to see Casey in front of the mirror. I hadn't heard anyone come in. I tell her hello then make a pretense of washing my hands so it looks like I was in the stall for a reason.

"You didn't flush," she tells me.

Then I sort of laugh. "Actually, I didn't need to." Then I look at her more closely and decide I might as well make her day. "I went in there to pray."

Well, her eyes just bug open. "To pray?"

I nod. "Yep. I invited God into my heart in church yester—"
But I can't even finish my sentence before she throws her arms
around me and hugs me so tightly that I almost can't breathe.

"Praise God!" she finally says as she steps back.

"Uh, yeah," I say, thinking that it might've been a mistake to
tell her.

"So what about this rumor that's going around school?" she
demands. "Did you and Justin really—"

"It's a lie," I cut her off. "Not that it's anyone's business. But just
so you know, it's a big fat lie."

"Well, that's a relief." Now she studies me carefully, like she's siz-
ing me up. "Because God really has something better for you, Zoë."

"Man, I sure hope so." Then I kind of laugh and take a nervous
step toward the door.

"And since you told me you're a believer I'm going to spare you
from my regular sermon," she says.

"Hey, I appreciate it."

Then we leave the bathroom and walk into the auditorium
together. Naturally, this invites some snickers (and I'm sure lewd
jokes) from Todd and Justin who are standing down by the stage
watching us. *Well, let them,* I'm thinking as I walk right past. I might
as well get used to it.

Thankfully, Nate is already backstage and I am relieved to hang
with him during most of rehearsal. And I'm beginning to notice
something happening among the cast. It's like these lines are being
drawn. Not with everyone. But definitely with some of us. Like somehow Shawna has formed this alliance with Todd and Justin now. Of
course, I realize this must appear more acceptable since Emily actually broke up with Todd on Saturday night. A huge relief to me personally. Of course, Emily is still totally bummed and not the least bit

pleased that she has to get tested for the STD this week. And on the other side of the line I find myself standing with Nate and Casey. Kind of weird. I mention this to Nate, but he assures me that he doesn't see it that way. "It might seem like it right now," he tells me as we wait for our next scene. "But, really, Zoë, they're not the enemy."

I nod and try to understand this, but I have to admit that Nate seems way ahead of me in these things. Still, I've decided to trust him on this. And I'm trying really hard to just act normal and go through rehearsal like everything's okay.

But then Justin makes this totally skanky comment about me (suggesting that I need to take lessons in performing an act that I have no intention of doing with anyone!) and I so really want to let him have it. But before I have a chance to say something, Nate steps in. "There's no need to talk like that," he tells Justin in a calm voice.

"How would you know?" Justin challenges him, and suddenly I can tell everyone is listening.

"Because Zoë is my friend. And what you said isn't true."

Justin laughs. "You mean Zoë hasn't done *that* for you, old man? Hey, you're missing out. She might be an amateur, but you probably wouldn't even know the difference."

Now Nate is looking seriously aggravated, and I want to smack Justin in the nose. "It's too bad that you have to make yourself feel better at the expense of someone else," says Nate.

"Hey, she gets what she deserves." Justin sneers at Nate now. "And I guess she deserves a geek like you."

Okay, Christian or not, there's only so much a girl can take. "Get over yourself, Justin," I say in a loud voice as I step right up to him and look him in the eyes. "Look, I'm sorry I upset you because I didn't want to have sex with you on Saturday night. But you don't have to take it out on Nate. If you were half the guy that Nate is, you wouldn't go around telling everyone a bunch of lies to cover up the fact that there's at least one girl in this school who isn't interested in sleeping with you."

"Two!" yells Casey, which almost makes me laugh.

Then Justin narrows his eyes and grabs me by the arm and says, "You got off easy, little girl. But you might not be that lucky next time."

"Next time?" I repeat. "There's not going to be a next time." Then I try to pull away. "Let go of me, Justin!"

But he doesn't.

"Let go of her," says Nate in a calm but firm voice.

Still Justin holds on. And he is squeezing hard.

"You're hurting me!"

"I said *let go!*" says Nate as he gets in Justin's face and puts a hand on his arm.

"That's right," says a loud voice behind us. I turn to see Mr. Roberts. "Let go of her, Justin."

Justin finally releases my arm and I rub the spot that's now throbbing.

"And you are excused from practice," says Mr. Roberts. Then Justin just turns and storms off. Most of the cast claps now.

Then Mr. Roberts takes Nate and me aside and demands an explanation. Feeling embarrassed, I tell him in general terms what happened and Nate backs me up.

"You kids," says Mr. Roberts in exasperation. Then he follows up by giving the rest of the cast a little lecture on how he expects us to act during the next several weeks of rehearsals. Finally, he says, "You know I can shut the whole thing down right now. And, yes, we'll lose money and we won't be able to do much in drama next year. But if you kids can't behave with a little self-respect and propriety"—he gives Shawna and Todd a firm look—"then we might as well cut our losses right now."

To my surprise, he seems to have everyone's attention and I'm hoping that this speech might help things to settle down around here. I'd hate to see our production canceled just because a few kids can't keep their hands off each other.

twenty-one

TO MY RELIEF, THINGS DO SETTLE DOWN FOR THE *OKLAHOMA!* CAST DURing the next couple of weeks. And for me personally. Justin and I have this sort of unspoken agreement to rehearse as needed and then avoid each other completely during the rest of the time. And it seems to be working. Still, I find myself totally amazed that I ever fell for that guy. Mostly I thank God that I didn't fall completely. Not that I think God wouldn't have rescued me from something worse. I'm just glad that he didn't need to. And, looking back at that time, I realize that both Nate and Casey were really praying for me, and I honestly think that God was looking out for and protecting me, not just from Justin, but from myself too. And that's pretty awesome.

Now today is Valentine's Day and I could be feeling all sorry for myself since I seem to be the only one on the planet without a boyfriend. Well, I do tend to exaggerate. But within my old group of friends it seems that everyone is neatly paired off, including Thea, who is now dating Justin (they probably deserve each other). But I have to admit that it really disturbed me when Emily and Todd got back together. Go figure! I guess she thought that since she tested negative for the STD everything was okay between them. "Don't worry," she said when I questioned her. "I'm being very careful now."

Well, I have no response to that. But I am definitely praying for her.

But as I was saying, today is Valentine's Day and it seems like everyone is acting all lovey-dovey and sweet and gooey, and here I am and I don't even have a boyfriend. But the thing is, *I am totally cool with that.* Everything's just fine.

Okay, I'll admit that I really like Nate *a lot,* and our friendship has steadily grown during the past several weeks. But we've both agreed that neither of us is ready to date. Not yet anyway. So we've decided to just be friends. Really good friends. And that's okay. In fact, it's better than okay. It's awesome!

But here I am in the locker room again, and the girls are all blabbing on and on about the Valentine's Dance, or more specifically what they'll be doing *after* the dance. It seems that several of the guys have rented hotel rooms so they can party on even after the band goes home. Now this used to be a custom reserved for prom night, but it's clear from what I'm hearing that some people will use any dance as an excuse to "get some."

Anyway, I for one am getting totally disgusted with the raunchy conversation in here, and I am seriously considering pulling a Casey Renwick on them, although it wouldn't be completely sincere because I haven't given up on guys entirely (although I am definitely saving myself for marriage!). I might like to date someday, especially someone as nice as Nate.

So after a particularly bad joke about edible undies, I just completely lose it. "Why don't you put a sock in it, Thea?" I say as I dangle a sweaty PE sock in front of her face.

She blinks then says, "Well, ex*cuse* me, little Miss Manners."

"What's up with you, Zoë?" demands Kirsti. "Don't tell me you're jealous. Are you feeling bad that Thea got your guy?"

I roll my eyes at her. "Yeah, you bet."

Now Thea puts her arm around my shoulders. *"Poor Zoë.* You don't have a date tonight, do you? Hey, maybe you should join Justin and me. We could have a sweet little threesome." She chuckles. "If ya know what I mean."

Now I realize I'm a Christian and I should have more self-control, but this just really irks me. "That is so sick." Then I wonder why I even bothered to open my mouth, since I am now the center of attention and it's not really working for me. But suddenly I have an idea.

"But you know what?" I continue talking in what I hope is an intriguing tone. "I do have a little announcement I'd like to make."

"What?" demands Kirsti.

I can tell they're all listening. "Do you guys remember when I told you about my surfer dude last summer? How we did it on the beach and everything?" Now Kirsti and Thea nod eagerly like maybe I'm about to give them another juicy tidbit. "Well, that was all just a big fat lie."

"I *knew* it," says Kirsti in a triumphant voice. "I *knew* you made that guy up!"

"And you know what else," I continue in a reckless way, knowing that I have their full attention now, "I am *still* a virgin."

Well, it's so quiet in the locker room that you can hear Mrs. Post's radio quietly playing oldies in her office. In fact, I wouldn't be surprised if she was listening too. But several of my friends are looking at me like they don't really believe what I just said. In fact, I can hardly believe I just admitted it myself.

"It's true," I continue. "And you know what else? I'm glad that I'm a virgin, and I don't care who knows about it. I don't even care if I'm the last virgin left in Hamilton High." Although I know this isn't the case since there's always Casey Renwick.

"Well, you're not," says a voice. And I look over to see Andrea standing up now. "Because I am a virgin too."

"No way!" says Thea, like she's getting seriously mad now.

"*Way.*" Andrea walks over and stands next to me. "I made it all up last year, just to get you guys off my case. But I'm sick of pretending." She takes my hand in hers then lifts them both like a victory sign. "Let the world know that I am a virgin too!" She's smiling now. "Just like Zoë. So get over it."

Then suddenly, to my total surprise, about fifteen other girls walk over and join us. Okay, they might not exactly be in our particular clique, but then who cares when it comes to virgin sisterhood? Because, one by one, each of them proclaims that they too are virgins. And pretty soon we are all just standing in this circle, laughing and slapping each other on the backs, and it is pretty clear that we are *not* a minority. I mean as wild as it seems, *virgins rule!* Well, at least in this particular class. I'm not sure about the rest of the school.

But I can't help but notice the "experienced" girls (like Thea, Kirsti, Shawna, and even Emily) watching us. And I can't help but think they look slightly out of it just now. Like maybe they're even regretting some of their choices or perhaps they're actually envious.

And before I start to gloat (which is seriously close to happening) I remember that I belong to God now. And I remember that my God is a gracious and forgiving God. And so I smile at the girls who are looking at us with expressions of slight bewilderment and I say to them, "But, hey, that's okay, you guys, I still want to be your friend."

Well, Thea and Kirsti just laugh at me like they think I'm totally nuts. And I suppose I was trying to be slightly funny. But I also notice this hopeful look in Emily's eyes, and maybe in Shawna's too. And I'm thinking, *Who knows what might come of this crazy confession?* And suddenly I can't wait to see what God will do next!

reader's guide

1. Early in the story, Zoë feels ashamed that she's still a virgin. Why? And why does she lie about it?

2. Zoë seems obsessed by the fact that she doesn't have a boyfriend. Why is her identity so wrapped up in this? What other qualities does Zoë have that might be more important?

3. Casey Renwick is hugely opposed to dating. How do you think she reached such a strong position?

4. Zoë talks to a number of people about sexuality. Who gave her the best advice? The worst? What would you tell her?

5. Zoë's parents seem a little checked out. Do you think that's good or bad? How involved are your parents?

6. What do you think Zoë should've done after discovering Todd cheating on her best friend? What would you do?

7. Zoë allowed herself to get into what could've been a date-rape situation. How could she have avoided this?

8. Who had the strongest influence in Zoë's life? Who has the most influence in yours? How do you feel about that influence?

9. Which character in *Torch Red* is the most like you and why? Do you wish you were like a different character? Why?

10. What do you think ultimately drew Zoë to make a commitment to God? What drew you to God? Or are you still searching?

TrueColors Book 4:
Pitch Black

Coming in September 2004

How does a girl climb out of the darkest depression of her life?

One

"DID YOU HEAR ABOUT JASON?" CARLIE'S EYES ARE WIDE AS SHE GRABS ME by the arm. But I'm just not in the mood for her theatrics right now. And I'm not interested in any juicy bits of gossip. Not even about Jason. And certainly not today.

I slam my messy locker shut. A sleeve of my favorite red sweatshirt is dangling out, hanging there like a panting tongue, begging to be rescued. But I just give the metal door a loud kick and turn away.

"Morgan!" Carlie is glaring at me now. "Listen to—"

"Just leave me alone!" I snap at her. "I'm going to be late for economics." Then I shake free from her grip and just walk away. Okay, I know I'm being totally rude. And Carlie is my friend. I should turn around and apologize. Friends don't treat friends like this. And, considering that my friends are pretty limited these days (like I can easily count them on one hand with fingers left over), I should really know better than to act like this. But the fact is I just don't care. Because this

is reality—my life sucks. And I am totally fed up. So everyone will be much better off if they just leave Morgan Bergstrom alone.

It's like I can't see anyone as I storm down the hallway toward the east wing. It's like I'm just walking down this dark tunnel and I'm fueled by anger. Oh, I can tell that kids are here and there, and maybe they're even looking at me. But I've got bigger problems to consider right now.

How can I be expected to get out of bed every morning and show up at this moronic school in order to get a stupid education (which is probably totally worthless) when everything in my life is totally out of control? I mean seriously, how much crud does a seventeen-year-old girl have to take? And it's not like this is my fault. I mean I've tried to do my best, to make good choices, and even be fairly responsible (at least for my age). But even so, it's like everything in my life just keeps falling apart. It's all unraveling and I just can't take it anymore.

Okay, it's no big deal that my parents got divorced when I was in grade school. I mean that happens to lots of kids. And eventually you get over it. And never mind that my older brother, Jonathan, is probably using drugs and my mom is totally oblivious. I mean he hardly ever comes home anyway. Although every time he does come home, something valuable goes missing. Last time he took my CD player. I now have a deadbolt lock on my bedroom door. But he's not really the problem either.

Okay, it bugs me that my mom doesn't really seem to notice these things lately. And even if I try to tell her, she's so preoccupied with her *own life* that she doesn't really listen. Oh, she pretends to listen, but you can tell by that glazed-over, dreamy look in her eye that she's off in La-La Land thinking about *Bradley*. Stupid, moronic Bradley Finch! Man, I wish she'd never met this loser dude from her job at the telephone company. They've only been dating a couple of weeks now, but it's like he's launched her into this ridiculous middle-aged pursuit of youth and superficiality that is not only totally embarrassing (I mean you should see what she's wearing these days!) but it's completely ruining my life. I mean talk about a train wreck! And it doesn't help anything that Bradley is in his twenties (he won't even tell us his real age) or that my mom is forty-three (which she won't admit to Bradley). She even told him that she'd had her kids when she was "just a kid" herself. Which is totally bogus, not to mention lame. But it's like she suddenly thinks she's Demi Moore and he's Ashton Kutcher and they are like the hottest couple in town. Give me a break!

At first, I told myself to just chill, that this whole thing would blow over before Valentine's Day. I mean most of my mom's romances don't last very long anyway, and this one seemed more doomed than the others. So I figured if I could keep my mouth shut and just be patient, things would eventually return to normal.

But now I know I was delusional. Last night those two idiots took their stupidity to a whole new level.

"We're getting married!" my mom announced from where the two lovebirds were snuggled up together on our couch. Now she said this like it was really good news, like I should jump up and down for joy.

"What?" I demanded, seriously hoping that I'd heard her wrong.

She smiled at me and laid a big wet one on Bradley. Then, giggling like she was in middle school, she turned back to me. "We're in love, honey. We've decided to get married."

"Married?" I actually gasped now. I mean it was one thing for them to date, and Bradley had already spent a few nights here in our apartment. But marriage? Give me a break.

"We love each other, Morgan. Can't you see that?"

"But, Mom . . ."

"I know, I know . . ." Mom smiled at me in this out-to-lunch sort of way. "It probably seems sudden to you. But we really want to do this."

"When?" I asked in a wimped-out voice.

"We're both taking off work tomorrow and Friday. We'll fly standby to Vegas, get married in one of those little chapels, and then spend the weekend there. Oh, can't you be happy for me, Morgan?"

I felt like I was going to be sick. "Mom?" I pleaded with her. "You can't be serious. I mean you guys barely know each other. And Bradley's, well, he's a lot younger than—"

"Oh, Morgan." My mom made her pouty face. "You know that age is just a number."

"But Mom, what about—"

"Hey, can't you just be happy for us, Morgan?" interrupted Bradley as he stroked my mom's recently bleached hair. "We belong together. Lee Anne is the best thing that's ever happened to me."

I wanted to suggest that perhaps Lee Anne could adopt him since I felt pretty sure she was old enough to be his mother.

"Whatever," I finally said. I mean what difference did my opinion make anyway? "I've got homework."

"So, you'll be okay, honey?" my mom called after me as I headed for my room.

"Yeah, I'll be fine." I could hear the dead tone of my voice. But I knew that she wouldn't even notice.

"And you don't mind being home by yourself for a few days?"

"Don't worry about me," I called as I closed the door to my room, securing the deadbolt even though Jonathan wasn't around. Then I threw myself on my bed and cried. I think I actually hoped that my mom might hear me and come in, like she used to do, and ask me what was wrong. I thought maybe she'd see how this was ruining everything and come to her senses, change her mind about marrying Bradley.

But she didn't. When I got up this morning, she was already gone. Her suitcases were gone. Her car was gone. And she didn't even leave a note telling me where she went or when she'd return. For all I know she may never come back at all. I'm not even sure that I would care if she didn't.

I glance around the classroom now, wondering how I even managed to get here and sit down. I can tell by the clock that this class is nearly over, and I don't even remember it starting. It's like I've been stuck in time, or maybe experiencing the *Twilight Zone*. But suddenly I remember that Carlie had been trying to tell me something about Jason. I look around the room to see where he's sitting. Maybe my pity party is coming to an end because now I feel slightly curious as to what Jason's up to. Maybe he finally got that tattoo. Wouldn't that freak his respectable, conservative parents? But I don't see Jason in class today. And suddenly I'm wondering if he's gotten into some new kind of trouble. I sure hope not since I'd really like to talk to him.

Jason and I have been friends since grade school. We even tried going out together when we were fifteen, but it felt too much like I was kissing my brother and so we called it quits. "Let's just keep on being good friends," I told him. And he agreed. And that's what we've done. In fact, I'm thinking that Jason is just the person to pour out my current problems to. He's a way better listener than Carlie. I mean even though he lives in this freaking, perfectionist world (with parents who are still happily married with great kids, and go to church every Sunday, and mow their lawn on Saturdays, and have respectable jobs, and impressive friends . . .) Jason is still totally understanding of my whacked-out little life. Maybe it's because he always considers himself to be the "black sheep" of his family. Which is totally ridiculous since Jason is one of the coolest guys I know. I mean he gets good grades, goes out for sports, hardly ever gets into trouble, and if he does, he's always sorry afterward. I mean he's not perfect, but compared to most kids he's pretty much got it together.

Of course, he doesn't see it that way. Sometimes he compares himself to his older brother and sister (who must be directly descended from God, they are so disgustingly perfect). But it's a lot to live up to, and sometimes Jason gets discouraged. And that's when he tends to do things, well, things that are not so smart. Things that he later regrets. Like the time he wrecked his dad's car drag racing down by the lake. Not a good scene. But he worked all summer to help pay off the deductible on the insurance, and eventually he even got to drive again.

Finally, class is over and I gather up my stuff, shove it into my backpack, and head for the door.

"Morgan," says Alyssa in a surprisingly sympathetic tone, especially for Alyssa, who can be a real witch sometimes. "How are you doing?"

I look at her and wonder if she's suddenly turned clairvoyant or nice or both. I mean how could she possibly know about my mom and Bradley? She's not even that close of a friend. "What do you mean?" I ask.

"I mean about Jason." She puts her hand on my arm and I feel an icy chill rush through me. Like I know something is wrong. Really wrong.

"What do you mean *about Jason?*" My voice sounds abnormally high-pitched now.

"You haven't heard?"

"*What's wrong, Alyssa?*" I can see other kids gathering around us now, like maybe they all know something that I don't. "What's wrong?" I say again. "What's going on?"

"Oh, I just assumed you knew." She looks uncomfortable now.

"About what?" My voice is getting louder.

She frowns. "Oh, Morgan, I hate to be the one to tell you."

I grab her by the arm now. "*Just tell me*, Alyssa. What is going on? What happened to Jason?"

"He, uh, he . . ." Her eyes dart to the other kids. "He killed himself last night."

I feel like someone has just sucked the oxygen out of my lungs, like I can't even breathe, or like I'm underwater and sinking fast. "No," I finally say. "That can't be true."

She nods. "I'm sorry, Morgan. I know you guys were close."

I turn and stare at the other kids, hoping they will straighten Alyssa out and explain to this ditzy chick that Jason Harding is alive and well, and that people shouldn't go around pulling crud like this. But their expressions seem to mirror Alyssa's. They all have this weird mixture of sadness and confusion and fear on their faces.

"No," I tell her again. "I don't believe you, Alyssa. If Jason was dead I would know it."

"It's been on the news," says Eric Stayton. "The whole school knows about it."

"I heard there's a special counselor to talk to kids," offers Eva Fernandez.

"Maybe you should go see him, Morgan," adds Alyssa.

They continue talking to me or at me or about me, I'm not even sure, but it's like I can't process what they're saying. It's like these heavy curtains have fallen over my eyes and my ears and I can't absorb what's going on around me.

Finally, I feel this hand beneath my arm and I am being guided somewhere. I try to take in a breath, try to steady myself as I attempt to walk down the hallway in a straight line. I turn to see that it's Eva next to me and she's talking to me as we walk. I don't really get what she's saying, but the tone of her voice is gentle and calming. And I'm hoping that maybe I've just totally misunderstood everything. I mean I realize that I wasn't thinking too clearly this morning, and I was really bummed about Mom and Bradley. Maybe I'm just having some sort of a breakdown where reality gets all twisted and distorted. Maybe I just need to take a nap or a pill, or throw cold water on my face.

Then we're in front of the office and I see this enlarged photo of Jason. It's his yearbook picture and it looks kind of grainy and uneven, but I know it's him. And beneath the photo is a computer-generated sign that says, "In Loving Memory of Jason Harding. We'll Miss You!" And beneath that is a long sheet of white butcher paper that goes all around the office wall. It has what appears to be graffiti all over it, but on closer inspection, I see that kids have written their names and things they remember about Jason.

And suddenly it becomes painfully clear. Jason really is dead. And it's like I'm the last one to know.

And then it's like my legs just totally give in and I collapse to the floor like a broken toy. I crumple into this pitiful heap of misery beneath Jason's enlarged photo and, right next to the office door where I hear phones ringing and voices talking, I burrow my head into my knees and sob. "Jason, come back," I beg. "Please, Jason, come back." I say these words again and again, thinking that maybe, if I say them enough or if I wish for it hard enough, just maybe I can undo this awful thing that's taken my friend away from me. But my world is turning black. Pitch black.

about the author

MELODY CARLSON has written dozens of books for all age groups, but she particularly enjoys writing for teens. Perhaps this is because her own teen years remain so vivid in her memory. After claiming to be an atheist at the ripe old age of twelve, she later surrendered her heart to Jesus and has been following him ever since. Her hope and prayer for all her readers is that each one would be touched by God in a special way through her stories. For more information, please visit Melody's website at www.melodycarlson.com.

OTHER BOOKS IN THE TRUECOLORS SERIES.

Brutally ditched by her best friend, Kara feels totally abandoned until she discovers these dark blue days contain a life-changing secret.
Dark Blue
Color Me Lonely
1-57683-529-4

Stuck in a twisted love triangle, Jordan feels absolutely green with envy. Things get so bad, Jordan even considers suicide, until her former best friend, Kara, introduces her to someone even more important than Timothy.

Deep Green
Color Me Jealous
1-57683-530-8

Following her friend's suicide, Morgan questions the meaning of life and death to come to her life's ultimate decision.
Pitch Black
Color Me Lost
1-57683-532-4
AVAILABLE IN OCTOBER.

1-800-366-7788
www.th1nkbooks.com